Anthony Vassiliadis is a young writer from Sydney, Australia. *The Highway Store and Other Stories* is his first book which he began writing at the age of 14.

I would like to dedicate this book to my mum, who has supported me in this endeavour the whole way—reading my drafts, spending days editing and most importantly, cooking for me.

Anthony Vassiliadis

THE HIGHWAY STORE AND OTHER STORIES

AUSTIN MACAULEY PUBLISHERS™
LONDON • CAMBRIDGE • NEW YORK • SHARJAH

Copyright © Anthony Vassiliadis 2023

The right of Anthony Vassiliadis to be identified as author of this work has been asserted by the author in accordance with sections 77 and 78 of the Copyright, Designs and Patents Act 1988.

All rights reserved. No part of this publication may be reproduced, stored in a retrieval system, or transmitted in any form or by any means, electronic, mechanical, photocopying, recording, or otherwise, without the prior permission of the publishers.

Any person who commits any unauthorised act in relation to this publication may be liable to criminal prosecution and civil claims for damages.

This is a work of fiction. Names, characters, businesses, places, events, locales, and incidents are either the products of the author's imagination or used in a fictitious manner. Any resemblance to actual persons, living or dead, or actual events is purely coincidental.

A CIP catalogue record for this title is available from the British Library.

ISBN 9781398482821 (Paperback)
ISBN 9781398482838 (Hardback)
ISBN 9781398482852 (ePub e-book)
ISBN 9781398482845 (Audiobook)

www.austinmacauley.com

First Published 2023
Austin Macauley Publishers Ltd®
1 Canada Square
Canary Wharf
London
E14 5AA

Credit for the cover illustration goes to Jacob Johnstone.

Table of Contents

Introduction	**11**
Prologue	**13**
Act 1: The Escapee	**17**
Act 2: The First Burial	**33**
Act 3: 'Skinhead' Sam and 'Jihad' Joe	**43**
Act 4: The Meeting	**62**
Act 5: Moonlight Reveries	**81**
Act 6: The Hitman	**93**
Act 7: Alice Springs	**103**
Act 8: Facing the Darkness	**113**
Act 9: The Sunset	**122**
Act 10: Giving Up the Ghosts	**129**
Epilogue	**140**
The Convention Centre Part 1	**143**
Journey	145
Part 2	**165**
Waiting	167

Part 3 **179**
    Home 181
    Watching 194
    There's a Man Following Me 197
    The Decision 205

Introduction

Along a highway stands a highway store. The only one for a 100 km, as the owner would love to tell you. Surrounding the store lies the seemingly endless outback. Ironically known as the bush, not that there is much flora besides the intermittent shrubbery and few wilting trees that always seem to survive, somehow. When your eyes set upon the store, it is almost impossible not to feel emotion. Not an architectural masterpiece by far or in the best shape (being a bit worn out) is the store. However, for some incomprehensible reason, it still evokes something. I guess you could call it nostalgia for the long-gone times of the '50s. Or maybe you could say the essence and character of the building does it for you. The store's awning juts out with the red italics standing out in bold, 'Trevor's Fuel and Snacks'. The store has a rusted tin roof, dingy yellowish-white pastel-coloured wooden walls and a wooden porch. Inside, the walls are the same as outside, except a darker toned colour. Inside, metallic shelves are stocked with the necessities for a long road trip, chocolate bars, Kangaroo jerky, chips, soft drinks, pies and more. Outside next to the porch stands the lone petrol-refuelling pump, styled in the classic '50s' way. And parked on the side of the building is the highway storeowner's ute, his 2012 HSV Maloo, as he was proud to say.

Prologue

His name was Trevor, he was 37 years old and already balding. He had a small potbelly that he wasn't happy about and wore his usual khaki pants. His sunburnt skin, dark brown, contrasted with the whiteness of his shirt. Trevor sat down on his folding chair, pulling out a beer from the esky. He looked out across the vast desert wilderness. The sun was beginning to set, not like it did in the cities, it was different out here. A flaming ball of vibrant saffron-yellow surrounded by splashes of red ochre. The wind gently nestled the chimes that hung from the door, creating a gentle tinkling sound. It took getting used to, even after a year, the complete absence of human activity. The nearest town was over 100 km away. There was the highway though, its asphalt cracked from years in the harsh sunlight. He must have been mad to buy the place. He had thought his store being the only place to get fuel and food for kms would make his business boom. Unfortunately, he couldn't have been more wrong. The new highway, 30 km back, which was more direct, had cut his business to the odd car once or twice a day. Damn—well, it could be worse he thought. And he'd had to get away from it all. The war had messed him up. Another of the bad choices in his life, signing up for the military. They don't tell you in the ads that you will see your friends get blown to pieces by shrapnel or the great guilt that comes with taking a life. He sipped on his beer—*that's right, drink your sorrows away, mate*, he thought.

He chucked empty can after can of beer off the side of the porch. His vision slowly dimming from the sides after each one. He remarked depressingly to himself about the pointlessness of his life. The fact that he never achieved anything! It always seemed like there was a deep, dark, gaping hole inside him—maybe he'd learn all 158 verses of the Greek National Anthem. That would fix the hole, solve his terminal depression. If the Japs could fix a sinkhole in two days, he could certainly solve one man's depression—surely. He'd read or watched somewhere that the power of positive thinking solved everything. He had to try that bullshit, what was there to lose? His dignity? Foam bubbled down his cheeks as he pondered this question. He decided it was pretty apparent that not much dignity was his to lose.

"Trevor, mate…you're a god. Y-ya know what, you're the best of the best, the cream of crop, the bing bang, bling blong…" He lost interest in this self-appraisal.

As usual, the pseudo-psychological theories of morons seemed to be as empty as…well, at the moment, he couldn't think of a good comparison. Maybe his soul? That seemed about right. Either way, the boffins of psychoanalysis seemed to be, as usual, inept in their 'efforts' to cure man's maladies of the mind. However, he was desperate, and he'd also heard another gem of wisdom—maybe this one wouldn't be tawdry. This pearl of wisdom, as he remembered it, was that devoting oneself to a purpose, a task, could solve depression. *Why not*, he thought, presently remembering his commitment to learning the Greek National Anthem. Maybe that would fill the hole in his life, such a noble aspiration! Surely, this task should fix him up, cover that hole! The hole that nothing could fix…he moped in a downtrodden way.

"Well, how does it start," he began. "Ahh yes. *Se gnorizo apo tin kopsi*," he uttered (more like chirped) in his lively Australian accent.

Even though he was a proud Greek, he knew he would never really commit to the effort of learning it. Even though he was an ashamed depressant, doing something about it was harder than drinking a beer. And with that, his hand shot for the esky, pulling out another Aussie psychologist. He liked this psychologist, he thought; he reckoned he better see them over and over. Really left you with a buzzing feeling in the tummy, he chuckled. And so that's what he did, he was a real regular. Beer after beer after beer, repeating the familiar tradition that had only been broken by a brief interlude of introspection.

He would wake up with a terrible hangover he thought, just before he blacked out.

***

The sun sparkled in his eyes, he felt at ease. Everything was perfect, a world in harmony. He smiled, his teeth glimmering. He looked across the vast desert, the light blue sky, his friends. He wasn't alone! He was one with nature. Then he saw a lone bikie driving towards his highway store. As the man got closer, clouds covered the sky. It wasn't sunny anymore but dark and gloomy. Now he was beginning to see the driver's face, something was wrong with it. The man's face was cadaverous; he looked sick. No, he looked dead. As the man got closer, it appeared that the skin slowly dissolved into his face revealing the man's bones. He was nearly at the shop now.

Act 1: The Escapee

A single motorcycle raced down the highway. Its Harley Davidson badge gleaming in the sunlight. Its engine roaring, a hungry beast eating up the kms. The sun gleamed on the man riding the motorcycle, reflecting off both the man's shades and sweat. The man's face was adorned by a beard surrounding his mouth and a prisoner's haircut. They'd got to his hair but never the beard, the man thought. He was clothed in leather everywhere, underneath the leather was an array of tattoos, one of which stood out. A viper and a knife on his arm, underneath it were two words, 'Viper Bikers'. His bulk protruded from every angle, or put less politely, the man was quite overweight, obese even on some metrics.

The man twisted the throttle, his idea had been a success. The fools had not expected him to take the old route, and even if they had tried to patrol it, his Harley got him out of Dodge too fast for them to do anything. He'd make it to Darwin tomorrow if he was lucky, he thought; he'd entered the Northern Territory two hours ago. It had been a big moment in his life when he crossed the border. He wasn't a particularly sentimental person, but he did realise that this was a turning point in his life. He'd never left South Australia before, and with the manhunt that was most likely going on down there, he might never return. So, he had turned over by the side of the road and had a VB. His last one at that. After the quick drink, he'd been back on the road. *No rest for the wicked,* he thought, laughing.

But damn that was a good escape, he thought, remembering his recent escapade fondly, a modern day Robin Hood he was. They couldn't catch him—though if they did, he always escaped. He fondly remembered his first escape, Mobilong! Though frankly it had been an insult, low security for him! Come on, he was a tough guy, a big timer. He deserved better, and he showed them. Breaking out in four months, but…they'd barely batted an eyelid. They hadn't seemed to have cared, no global manhunt, no nationwide one, not even a statewide one! Well, that was different this time, he'd finally gotten the recognition. He'd become a big timer in the Vipers, but they still hadn't noticed. Fucking hell…he was regional president. But when that fucking fag turned up, what was his name…something annoying. Robbie, yeah, something fucking dumb like that. The prick had come up from Sydney, acting like a fucking bigshot. Trying to incorporate his chapter into NSWs, saying it would be better for him! The balls on the man…well, he'd shown him. He shot him and two of his fuckhead lieutenants. Of course, they died, pretty painfully. He laughed. Anyways, the pigs took notice then, he was wanted number 1; he was more popular with the piggies than Milat. But the bastards caught him, sent him to Yatala. Finally, a bit of respect. They'd sent him to G-Division, aptly named. He definitely was a god, a legend of sticking it to the big state.

When he'd turned up to prison, a bit of a crowd had showed up. He'd been sure they'd been there to celebrate his exploits, his defiance of the state and of pricks like…Robbie, he'd remembered the bastard's name. Anyways, apparently the people had been there to shout at him! Apparently, they didn't like bikies! Shouting *wanker* and *you deserve to die in prison*—those fools were just working for the deep state. If he hadn't been in chains, he would have taught them a lesson. Anyways, he'd entered the prison a king, the castle's most famous resident, a bigger timer than Alan Bond. The man had beaten the big timers, been an underdog. Y'know running against the New York Yacht Club's 132 years of tyranny and winning. That, he respected, and for that crime, against the establishment, they'd sent him to prison. Made him out to be a criminal, that he was bankrupt. They just didn't like him going into media and becoming a big timer. Look, the man was an inspiration, and the fact that he was a greater hero than his hero filled him with pride.

He remembered his pappa had told him that one day he could be as great as that man, and he'd been right. Though the state had persecuted him for his truth telling, hunted him like a dog! But that hadn't stopped his daddy's sermons. Man took it on his shoulder and had fun. Running from the authorities, he'd loved that, that was his cricket. He was a professional, and he'd loved it too. Father and son escaping the clutches of Hawke, what could be better? They had fun—but sometimes, he got angry; it was just the pressure of the state, he told himself. Else Father wouldn't have hit him. He was a good man, a great man, but great men have to vent! Have to teach. And he'd learned! Violence the key to a man's toolbox. Maybe one day it wouldn't be needed—maybe. But what the hell, he wasn't a pussy. And it was right, who was to say he couldn't bash someone's head in. God? Well, Father had certainly had thoughts on the big man; whenever he saw a church, he would burst into a rant. Every church, every priest, every page of the bible, the tools of the deep state to control the people, he had said. And really, it had made sense to him. A lot had made sense to him back then…Unions were devils, devils were fairy tales told by the deep state to scare us into submission, but the deep state and in particular the police were undeniably devils. Marxists were mad, fascists fuckheads, liberals log heads, conservatives cunts. All this had made sense back then, now he wasn't so sure. Sometimes, he'd even caught himself wishing he was just a normal Aussie man, with a nice family, house, accounting job—but that was just weakness, the deep state's brainwashing. He'd once asked Father to go to school and was promptly and rightly beaten. He'd asked for a normal life, well, at least insinuated it and surely been righted. Whenever he had these sacrilegious thoughts, he promptly flagellated—the wisdom of his father ever implemented to this day.

Discipline, utter unthinking trust were important. *Weakness begets subjugation. Violence begets strength.* He remembered his father's words, focussed on them …his doubts would pass. The divinity of his struggle would soon be proven. They didn't see it now; they saw him as a petty criminal! But he was more than that, he was a rebel. The Vipers…sure they were a 'criminal organisation' but through them he was fighting the state. It didn't matter how much blood was spilt, it was surely right. He was Robin Hood—but maybe he didn't want to be anymore. Maybe his fight was over. Maybe he could just disappear and…but he couldn't, he wouldn't, he had to destroy the state that had destroyed his father.

He remembered they'd been running for months. It had been 1985. That was the year the state really took his father seriously. People had been flocking to his father at the time, so many scared and disillusioned. Rightly so, people were out of jobs, and the worst of the worst, the USSR and USA were on the edge of nuclear war. So, his father shot to the limelight, and none of the big shots liked it. They despised his father—because they, the deep state, felt threatened. They accused his father of being involved in crime, with the Vipers, and they accused him of inspiring riots and civil unrest. So they came for him, so he ran. They had escaped, even managed to enjoy it for months, but each month, they got closer—each month, he got angrier. And then on that final day, they had surrounded the motel. There was so much shouting. His father had pulled out a gun and pointed it to his head.

He'd said, "I'll shoot the kid's brains out if you take one more step."

He knew he hadn't meant it, but then, they took one more step and—he pulled the trigger. But nothing happened, the gun had jammed. But they still shot him.

They took him away for re-education in foster care, but he knew what the state was trying to do so he continually ran away. They said he was a defective—dumb, uneducated, hopeless, but he knew those were just the labels they used on revolutionaries. As soon as he could, he joined the Vipers; he didn't know how old he'd been then, his father had never held a birthday for him. But who needed birthdays? The Vipers raised him, showed him that through the Viper's he could fight against the state and avenge his father. He knew that by dealing drugs he was slowly destroying the state's hold on the minds of the people. He knew by robbing and killing those with flashy cars, he was helping the needy. He knew he was renowned as Robin Hood, that each of his exploits was a fabled tale. He knew he couldn't wait for his next escape—though now he wasn't so sure. Nowadays, nothing was black and white.

Anyways, thoughts like these were not healthy, he reminded himself. He had to, he had to stay strong! So…he remembered his escape—that was a classic. It'd be a movie one day, that was for sure. He'd planned it for months; he'd had time to think, lots of time in solitary, too much time. And as he knew, too much time thinking was a bad thing. So he'd devoted his existence to escape. In passing, he'd seen a former comrade there, he'd been sent to solitary for a fight. Luck had been on his side and they'd been placed next to each other. They had been able to talk through the windows at the back of each cell. He'd convinced the man to organise a riot; he'd planned it all in his head and it was genius. A fire would be lit in solitary, this would cause the evacuation of prisoners in section G. This would be timed to coincide with leisure time outside for the other inmates. When the latter would riot, the sheer chaos would overwhelm the prison guards. He would break from the evacuation and steal the prison guard's Harley (which he constantly bragged about, knowing full well he was being heard by one very unhappy bikie). So, all had gone to plan, somehow Section G had been set on fire, the explanation he had set on were that prisons were prisons. A few criminals had become crispy chicken, but he didn't feel one bit sorry, one was a serial killer, the others he wasn't sure about. But he had no sympathy for those animals, they just wanted death with no meaning—unlike himself, unlike his noble cause? At least, he hoped so. So as the overwhelmed guards dealt with a riot, the dickhead guard tried to lead the surviving criminals out of the block. But when he dropped the keys—he laughed at this knowing full well the old adage about dropping things in a prison—he'd jumped him. Bashing his head against the side of the cage, he had then got the keys, opened the door, which had been a bit of a challenge cuffed, and had then run for the wind. Some of his fellow escapees got bashed by the guards; he remembered seeing one guy's teeth getting smashed out by a baton, but soon, the whole prison was being overwhelmed. In the courtyard, the guards in riot gear fought vainly against hundreds of very angry prisoners, but he had had a plan unlike those fools. He knew where to go, because the now very dead guard had been stupid enough to continue to shout it out. He went to the carpark and took the man's Harley (the idiot had been stupid enough to leave the keys in the ignition). So he raced out just as the whole Adelaide police department seemingly turned up, racing off down the highway towards Darwin. But that was not before he had run, at his own risk, to the prisoners' possessions office to retrieve his gear; he would not leave without his jacket, let alone his sunglasses. He'd pulled at drawers, savagely searching for his belongings, and in the process discovered some VBs, which he was almost as happy to find as his belongings.

His thoughts were interrupted by red flashing from the fuel gage. *Fuck*, he thought, *where was he supposed to get fuel around here?* He looked into the horizon, hoping he would see the familiar Caltex or 7 Eleven sign. He knew he couldn't walk—if his bike conked out, he was a goner. He'd either be taken by the desert or by the cops, who would surely be sending someone down this highway eventually. However, just when all hope seemed to be gone, he saw it. It was divine, even though he did not believe in such things, 'Trevor's Fuel and Snacks, 5 km away, you'll love our prices'. He never thought he'd be this happy to see a billboard. The edges of the billboard were weathered; its white paint peeling and its bold red lettering beginning to fall off. But that made it no less angelic. He hoped the place was still around though, it sure looked weary and decrepit, but then again, everything in this world was looking that way nowadays. He saw a mob of kangaroos running by the side of the road. Enjoying their freedom, just like he was. They'd never take his freedom away again; he'd make sure of that.

He continued down the road, he'd make it, he thought. Only 4 km left, 3 km left, 2 km left. But at 2 km, his Harley stopped, never to start up again. At first, it jittered, and he had hoped it might get going again. But unfortunately for him, it did not start up again.

"C'mon, you bastard, just 2 km left."

He turned the throttle roughly, but nothing happened. It was truly dead.

"You absolute piece of shit!" he screamed.

In a fit of rage, he began to smash the motorcycle. Punching, kicking and even jumping on the thing. The numerous psychologists he'd seen over the years had always said he had anger issues, but that had always only made him angrier. However, he did take a bit away from those sessions, take a deep breath and another and you'll calm down. Unfortunately for the Harley, he only began these exercises after decimating it. He slowly began to cool down, figuratively at least, because his recent outbreak of furore had raised his body temperature sky high, the last thing you wanted under the circumstances.

He looked down at the miserable wreck of the Harley and fought the urge to blow up again. He didn't need to get any warmer than he already was and blowing up wouldn't achieve anything. But damn, it felt good, he thought, smiling and taking one last kick at the bike. As usual, violence was king.

Fuck it, he'd have to walk, he thought bitterly. Not something he liked doing very much, as evidenced by his physique. Though at least he could go to the servo and get help, but the bloody heat! The 2 km wasn't much of a distance, just down the road, but in this weather, it was a fucking marathon. He began his trek, after 500 m, sweat was already streaming down his face. He chucked off his leather jacket and threw it to the ground. He loved it, but in the heat, he just couldn't wear it. He looked around him, he could see the heat wavering in the air. It was like he was in a microwave. *A little fucking piggy, getting cooked*, he thought. He looked into the distance, but his vision wasn't good enough to make out much. All he could see was a road and red sand everywhere.

As the sun continued, its relentless attack upon his body and sunstroke set in, mental fatigue overwhelmed him. Already not the most mentally stable man this spurred delusion and mania. *Maybe the bastard cops had planned this all along*, he thought, *maybe their plan was for him to die in the desert. And what the fuck was with that Servo owner, keeping his shop 2 km away from him? He was obviously in on it too! The place probably didn't even exist. He'd kill the person who owned the place if it didn't exist; he'd bash his head in. That'd teach him a lesson about collaborating with the cops.*

***

Trevor was awoken by the clamour of a madman. He sat up from his chair and vomited, his hangover had been worsened by the sudden shock. He looked forward and saw the man coming towards his shop, his body red, his movements sudden. Trevor got up and ran to the man; he looked as if he was about to drop dead. As he got closer, he could make out some of the man's senseless blabber. Words like 'kill' and 'gonna kill them' stood out to him. Not being an idiot, Trevor reasoned, he thought it sensible to stop several metres away from the man and call out to him. He didn't know what he was dealing with here, the man could be a psychopath.

"You okay, mate?" asked Trevor.

The mad bikie did not answer him but continued his approach towards him; with every movement the man made, it seemed he was lurching forwards. Trevor marvelled at the fact that the man hadn't stumbled over yet.

"Look, what happened to you? Can I help you?" asked Trevor tentatively, taking a step back.

He continued to approach him, each step forwards the madman took, Trevor mimicked with one backwards. Trevor had been repeating this process without thought, like a robot, to such a successful degree that he did not notice the step behind him and tripped backwards. The wooden steps sent splinters into his arms when he tried to break his fall. He knew at that instant that he should have maintained them better, so as not to have endured the pain he felt now. Another mistake in a long line of ones that littered his life.

"Fucking hell!" Trevor screamed in agony.

He had endured a gunshot wound in Iraq, but the pain of a splinter always got him. *To be fair*, he thought, *it got everyone*. He had been so preoccupied with the splinters that he forgot about the madman who was now only inches away from him. It seemed his recent, quite vocal, outburst of pain had alerted the man to his presence. He looked up and saw the man looming over him. They locked eyes and Trevor finally knew who he was dealing with. In the man's eyes, he saw pure mania, he had seen it before. That look. That pure absence of rationality. The last time he had seen it, many had died.

***

The year was 2014, the country Afghanistan. Corporal Trevor Jones, as he was known then, had led his section into the NATO-controlled village of Idak Hashwari. There had been reports of Taliban activity inside the village, so his section had been sent to investigate. He had argued with his superiors saying that they needed at least two sections from the unit to properly investigate while maintaining mission safety. However, they had refused.

So, they went in undermanned into what was possibly now a hostile village. It was never going to turn out well, the inquiry resolved later. As they approached the village, foreboding grew inside Trevor. He knew, somehow, that something bad would happen if they entered the village, but he had his orders. His men had the same feelings just as he did, but they knew the repercussions of refusing an order too—a court martial and a prison sentence. This didn't stop them from complaining incessantly. Or possibly, it was the opposite. Their lack of cheerful banter and light-hearted complaints creating an atmosphere of solemnity and trepidation. Something that was so much worse. What he could remember clearly was Private Singh's remark, a remark that truly epitomised the whole situation. That put into words what everyone was thinking. "There's bad juju in this village, Corporal. We shouldn't enter because if we do, I don't think we'll ever come back!"

Trevor noted the surrounding mountains on either side of the village. *Great spots for snipers*, he thought. *We'll be sitting ducks.*

But what was the difference, he thought, *the whole war had been a shit show, nothing here was different. Still blockheads who didn't know a thing were running the war and grunts like himself dying for it.* He looked around at his surroundings, no longer the alert corporal but a contemplative tourist. This rugged paradise could have been beautiful, but it was a hellhole, those prodigious picturesque mountains a perfect hiding spot for men wishing the death of every man he led here today. So, he ditched the tourist mentality, the tourist who took in the great beauty of this place, and returned to the alert corporal. The loyal corporal, the corporal with an unblemished record…but neither was completely true these days.

As they entered the village, Trevor noticed that it seemed completely deserted; it was looking more and more like an ambush.

"Okay, men, be on guard, we could have a situation here," he said.

"Is anyone here?" shouted Private Smith.

No answer.

"C'mon, you bastards, where are you?" shouted Private Smith.

"Looks like no one's here. I think we should leave, Corporal," said Lance Corporal Wilson.

"No, we can't. We've got explicit orders to make sure there is no Taliban in the village. We'll have to clear the buildings."

"The place is empty, C'mon we should leave; I don't like it here. It would be perfect for a trap."

"Calm down, Robert, I'm sure it's safe here. The villagers are probably having a festival at some other village, you know how they have those things. Think of this as a blessing, with no one in the village we can freely search the buildings without the risk of one of them catching onto what we are doing and aaliyah akbaring him."

"Yeah, I guess you're right," Lance Corporal Wilson said, laughing nervously.

"Okay, men, fall out, two per house, let's get this done. Rendezvous here in 30 minutes. The lance corporal and I will be on lookout," he ordered.

Trevor watched as his men went into the houses, holding their assault rifles in front of them. Each as nervous as the other. It seemed the atmosphere of fear would not stop rising. He rested upon the town well's side. He would be glad when this mission was over. However, that mission never really ended for him, he reminisced. Even when he got back home, he'd close his eyes and be back there. As he sat there resting against the wall, he smelt it, that horrible smell, that smell he would never forget. He turned around and peered down into the well. He had found where the villagers had gone.

"Everyone out now!" he screamed in vain, too late.

Explosions began to rack the village as buildings blew up. He could remember the screams of his men vividly. And as he got up to try and do something, he just froze. He'd seen combat before, but this was different, this was just a slaughter. The lance corporal was screaming, asking what the orders were, but he could not reply. It was as if time was moving rapidly forwards, but he was frozen in the past, unable to do anything. At this moment, he saw the man with mania in his eyes. The man was a suicide bomber, and he was running towards him. Trevor locked eyes with him and knew that there was nothing he could say or do to stop the man from what he was about to do. There was no reason or sense in those eyes. He saw, as though watching a film, the lance corporal run towards him. And as the lance corporal turned back to look at Trevor one last time, he saw that sad look on the man's face. He was going to go home in a coffin and Trevor on a plane. He'd never see his family again and Trevor would go home to see no one. He never knew why the lance corporal did it and he never would. The lance corporal jumped on the jihadist and was no more. Engulfed in a ball of fire, obliterated with nothing left to bury.

He'd left the military after that and never looked back again. Since that day, he had abhorred violence, enough people had died for one lifetime. He had pledged from that day onwards he would not kill again.

***

A tear rolled down Trevor's face as he looked up in solemnity, knowing violence was to soon blight his peaceful recluse. Everything was silent and everything was peaceful, dust began to swirl, and the store creaked. Trevor would have laughed if the situation was not so serious. Everything about what was going to go down was perfect, the whole scene picturesque, it was a duel. And then, the peace was broken.

"Die you bastard!" screamed the madman, leaping onto Trevor.

Trevor felt the air rush out of his lungs, as the impact of the man's landing hit him. The man grappled for Trevor's neck, trying to use his larger bulk to stop him from struggling. Unfortunately for him, he had not bargained on fighting a man with combat experience. Trevor pushed his knee upwards, getting the man in his Harry Daniels (or 'The Man's Testicles' as his ninth-grade teacher insisted were the proper way to refer to them).

"Mother fucka!" yelped the madman in anguish.

The man recoiled in pain, groping his balls. While Trevor got up shakily, still feeling the impact of the man's landing, the madman looked at Trevor with pure hatred. Now it was not just mania, but Trevor's attack on the man's baby makers that seemed to have given the man a justification for assaulting him. Trevor did not know which was worse, a maniac after you for no reason or one who had a reason.

"My mum always said I was good with balls," mocked Trevor.

"You're so dead, I'll kill you so dead that they'll have to mercy kill you!" the man shrieked. At this point, Trevor just stared at the man in awe. His unique ability to come up with such a paradoxical statement so quickly impressed him. Then he realised the man was obviously an idiot.

"Look mate, you're obviously not in a good mental state, probably have sunstroke bad by the look of you. You need some medical help (and some mental too, he thought). I can drive you," pleaded Trevor, attempting to appeal to the man's sanity, hoping the man had some left. He was surprised at his own generosity though; the man had tried to kill him and he was offering to drive him to a doctor! However, he knew his plea would be pointless, he had seen the man's eyes, there was no reason in them.

There are moments in one's life that will define the rest of it. Whether to move country, marry that girl or something as simple as accepting someone's help. Take this instance, for example. The madman accepted Trevor's help, his offer to drive him to the hospital, and he was treated both physically and mentally. Trevor and the man formed a friendship and are friends to this day. The End.

"Die!" screamed the madman.

The madman attempted to get up, but before he could, Trevor tackled him. The two men, two alive men, landed on the ground. Ten seconds later, there was only one man alive.

Act 2: The First Burial

Trevor punched the man in the face, again and again. He hadn't noticed the trickle of blood that was seeping from underneath the man's head, just as he hadn't noticed the small, pointy rock that he had tackled the man into. The man's eyes stared blankly at him, this should have alerted him to the fact that something was wrong, but in the heat of a fight, common sense can often be lost. Everything for that matter can become distorted. So, for that reason, Trevor decided to hit the now deceased madman in the Huevos. *This is sure to make him respond*, he had thought.

So, Trevor punched him in the family jewels and finally realised what had happened. When Trevor first made contact with the man's private area, two things happened. First, Trevor was shocked by how wet the area was. Second, the force of the punch moved downwards, disturbing the faeces that were in his pants. This created a squelching noise.

Trevor saw the man unmoving, saw that he had emptied his bladder and guts and saw his eyes wide open, not crazed now but shocked. He realised the man was dead. That he had killed another man. Something he wished he'd never have to do again, something he'd *pledged* he would never do again.

"Maybe you're still alive, c'mon please, oh God," he said, wishing that by saying it, it would come to be.

Then he saw the blood and knew there was no chance; he already knew it in his head, but he had refused to truly accept it. *No*, he thought to himself. *NO!* Why had he done this, why had he killed a man? He remembered his oath, his pledge, his promise not to kill. He remembered a quote from Shakespeare, the only one he remembered, so fitting, so perfect that it almost felt like it had been written for this moment. 'For oaths are straws, men's faiths are wafer-cakes'. And in this instance, he knew it was so true; he had promised, *pledged*, not to do violence again, not to kill and yet he broke that promise. Like so many others he had broken throughout his life. He had promised to protect his men; he had promised to protect Alicia. He had…

He got up and started walking backwards anxiously. He felt dirty, felt criminal. This wasn't Iraq or Afghanistan, killing a man who came after you would result in an investigation. He felt like running away and hiding but knew he couldn't. "You're not the criminal," he told himself. He repeated this multiple times in his head, and in those minutes after his realisation, it became his new mantra. A mantra that was absolutely infallible, until he realised most people in prison probably had the same mantra. He took a deep breath and knew what he needed to do. He needed to have a beer.

He was using the old military technique he'd learnt many years ago, to deal with the mental pain of killing a man. 'Have a few beers and tell yourself that the person you killed was 'the bad guy'. At least, he still *felt*. He knew that now. There were many he knew that didn't *feel* anymore. They could kill a guy and not even shed a thought about it.

Five minutes later, he heard the satisfying 'pop' of the beer bottle. He chucked the bottle opener away and downed the beer in a minute.

"Well, I'll have to bury him then," he exclaimed nonchalantly, psychologist Beer having done the trick yet again.

He walked over to the now deceased madman and began to drag his body around the back. In the process, blood continued to leak from the madman, creating a stream of blood as Trevor dragged him along. The blood weaved its way through the gravel and spread throughout the dirt. A grotesque river of blood; he knew he'd have nightmares about it. There was something so horrid and unnatural about it, but he'd seen it before. And just like then, everything had gone downhill from there. That vermillion river; so wicked in its radiance, so thick and rich and deep, coagulating as the eye of the devil.

He could almost laugh at this miscreation of his. There was such a cruel irony in it, streams, rivers, water in general, were supposed to bring rejuvenation, new life. All this river brought was death and more death. But that was not the true punchline, no, that was even more hilarious. Why he'd tried so hard to escape death, to get away from it, to prevent it! But all he'd done is walk right up to the doorstep, ring the doorbell, and open the door. But he wondered—hoped? When would the day come when he would be pulled inside that dark doorway? If he was a boat, then this was his river. This repugnant ode to his life. Blood, blood, blood! He just wondered when he too would finally be devoured by it. Though maybe he already was.

But even as his melancholy burgeoned, the sweet refrain of manual labour took its toll and Trevor momentarily forgot his broodings on death and his dolour. The sun beat down on him as his unnurtured arms battled to drag the brick that was once a man. What was once regret turned to genuine annoyance at the man having died. As any psychologist would tell you, even a man in his greatest state of self-loathing will always blame another when confronted with some arduous chore. These condemnations will usually be accompanied by some, unknown until now, language skills in French, uttered by said man. Trevor was no exception to this rule, each pull of the bikie, now dubbed ogre, was met by some obscenity. Although what was being conducted was by no means a usual chore, chore being liberally defined in his male psyche as really referring to any instance in which a man does not want to do something; such as meeting the in-laws, doing the dishes, cleaning and in particular, the dreaded, remembering the anniversary (and the expected organisation of something special for it). But for most, the latter can be quite difficult, and to follow the usual procedure of blame, swear and do the littlest would be quite unadvisable.

Some brave souls have tried the usual routine of blaming someone else, one's name was Henry. Some historians suggest this man's actions were the trigger for the establishment of the Church of England.

Finally, after an excruciating seven minutes of work, the deed was done. *The man had to weigh a tonne*, Trevor thought. With this thought, memories of a science lesson were triggered. Some underpaid and overworked teacher, with rather ridiculous hair, was instructing an uninterested class (including himself regretfully) about the 'fascinating' fact that all objects had gravity. For example, if a man fell out a window, he would be pulled to earth, but the earth would also be pulled towards him (of course just before he went splat). Trevor wondered, for a flicker, if his choice of analogy indicated a serious problem in his psyche; he would let this one go though, knowing full well another onslaught of introspection would not bode well for his sanity. Especially given he was rather certain on the outcome of such a venture. Anyways, he thought, so it was a scientific fact that everything had gravity. He looked at the dead body, the rather large dead body. *How old was he? Forties*, he reckoned. *And when did climate change become a big thing? He may have solved the problem!*

Trevor, having yet again lost himself in his thoughts, found himself standing next to the side of the store holding the dead man's body. Sweating incessantly by now, he dropped the body and knew what his next steps were. Five minutes later, and a beer in his hand, Trevor was digging the man's grave and possibly his own in this weather, he thought. As the hole grew deeper, so did his weariness. As his weariness grew, so the difficulty of digging ballooned. He tore off his shirt in desperation, lamenting the act instantly—he'd loved the shirt, even though it was plain white and boring, and he had a dozen more exactly the same.

As he dug more and more, he seemed to be digging himself deeper into sorrow. No longer was he able to brush off his sadness and laugh it off. He looked at the spade in his hand, pondering doing himself in with it, but the thought repulsed him. *How could he think this way? What right did he have to do such a thing? How unfair would it be? But would it be? Did he need to live to be punished, or for others?* Because he knew for certain that there was no one left that would cry when he died.

As these thoughts grew louder and louder, he threw the spade at the side of the wall and collapsed in sorrow. He should have acted differently! The man was obviously suffering from delusions brought on by the conditions, the inescapable, ineluctable heat that plagued the outback. His sympathy had been clouded by his damned hangover, something he was sure to wake up with again. He had not realised, truly grasped the man's condition, but now, he knew, which made it that much worse. His experience digging the man's grave had allowed him to understand the mental state of the man. Already, Trevor himself was feeling the symptoms that the other man had felt.

But his sudden outburst of remorse and sorrow was brought to a quick stop when he noticed the tattoo, one of many, on the man's arm. It had been dangling over the hole's edge for a while now, but he had not given the arm nor the tattoo a thought till now. The viper and knife insignia were familiar to him, as was the inevitable lettering underneath. 'Viper Bikers'! He remembered his girlfriend, Alicia. The moment he'd walked in and found she'd overdosed. The look of betrayal his brother had given him when the police had taken him away. Even though it had been night, the police sirens shining on his face had accentuated his features, all too clear.

This unwanted flood of memories continued to rush on. Trevor tried to banish them away by working harder, but exhaustion had already set in. He just exacerbated the problem and soon delusions overtook him, just like what had happened to the bikie.

He walked into the store, tilting from side to side perilously, looking for a can of white paint and a plank of wood; he couldn't remember how, but somehow he found it, and the next thing he knew, he was at the tree adjacent to the burial spot hanging a crude sign that read, 'Trev's Burial Yard for the dead or bastards like I like to say'. Trevor laughed maniacally at this. Next thing he knew, he was making a wooden plaque for the madman that read 'Dead Bikie (?–2020)' He laughed at this too. Then Trevor had completed this plaque and somehow buried the madman.

Suddenly he set off running blindly into the desert. As he ran shirtless, sweaty and sunburnt into the distance, he began howling. His screams akin to the mating calls of the kakapo. His crazed eyes, bloodshot, his hands red with blood, his hair uncombed, beard untrimmed, face gaunt, his whole appearance rabid. He ran towards a rocky outcrop and climbed it like a wolf, looked up at the sun and howled. His scream echoing for miles. He stood there searching wildly and then bounded off. Soon he crashed down into the dirt and passed out.

As he came back to consciousness, he found he was in the car of Officer Garry Walker, Gazza as he liked to be called.

"You bastard, you're lucky I decided to check on the locals 'cause of the weather, otherwise you'd be dead. What were you doing runnin' in the desert?"

"I don't know, guess it was the desert, you know how it gets to you!"

"More like the alcohol, I can smell it a mile away. You know the heat and alcohol don't mix well."

"Yeah, says you." Trevor pulled a beer out of Gazza's esky in the backseat.

"Bloody oath, mate, haven't you had enough?" Gazza laughed.

"You can never have too much beer."

"My oath, nothing like a cold one. Oi, can you pass us one here?"

"No probs," said Trevor passing Officer Walker a beer.

"I thought you were supposed to pull people over for drink driving?" said Trevor.

"Don't worry, I'll pull myself over in an hour," said Gazza, laughing hysterically.

Trevor remembered his bloody state and looked down but found the blood cleaned off.

"Don't worry about that, Trev, I cleaned you up. What'd you do…kill a kangaroo?" Trevor laughed.

"Yeah, something like that." Trevor laughed uneasily.

"Y'know when I found you, I thought you were fucking dead. Covered in blood, literal streaks of red down your face, bloodshot eyes. Checked your pulse and you were still alive, not so sure about your kidneys though, mate. So I cleaned you down, in fact you woke up at one stage. Vomited of course and then fell asleep again. Fucking sleeping beauty you were."

"And you didn't take me to hospital?"

"Hey, mate, I'm only a simple copper. Knew she'd be right. Crikey! I was still in shock about the whole thing."

Trevor looked at Garry's face, there was no suspicion there. He was a nice guy but not the brightest or most competent. He was thankful for that in this instance.

"By the way, Trev, I've been working on something you might like to see," said Gazza.

"What, mate?" replied Trevor.

"You'll see," said Officer Gazza, smashing his foot down on the accelerator.

The Holden Commodore zoomed forwards against the backdrop of the sunset. The Commodore's wheels kicked up dirt, creating an ochre cloud around it.

"What the fuck, Gazza!" screamed Trevor.

Officer Garry ignored Trevor, turning the wheel harshly to the left and right, kicking up even more dirt.

"You ready?" shouted Gazza.

"For what?" screamed Trevor hysterically.

"For this!"

Gazza spun the wheel around and around, pressing the brakes hard. The Commodore spun around in a donut elegantly, and then, with a sinister grin, Gazza decided to repeat the stunt on Trevor.

"You beauty!" screamed Gazza.

He proceeded to press down on the accelerator again and repeated the spectacle. Not once, no, but again and again.

From afar, a mob of kangaroos watched, their heads turning back and forth watching what they dubbed the 'bogan humans'. *What idiotic act were they committing now,* they wondered. Their ears turned up at the yelps of fright emanating from Trevor. They had never heard a human yelp that much and it unnerved them. Soon though, they became bored of watching the idiocies of man and bounced off to have dinner, leaving the two men all alone.

Sometime later, Trevor stumbled back into the highway store, followed by the taunts of Gazza.

"We should do this again; didn't you have fun?" shouted Gazza drunkenly.

Trevor turned back and watched as Gazza made his way back, swerving from side to side. Not intentionally this time, just drunkenly.

"They should give ya the Queen's police medal!" bellowed Trevor sarcastically.

Sadly, Trevor's great moment of tact was not heard by Gazza, a man either too drunk or too far away now to hear.

Trevor fell on his bed like a rock as soon as he was there, his last conscious thought, *I'm gonna wake up with a terrible hangover.*

***

In his dreams, Trevor dreamt that he was watching the news. The presenter was recounting a gruesome gangland war that had been fought between a group of neo-Nazis and jihadists. Everyone had been killed except for two, one from each despicable organisation, the presenter had said. Both were now on the run, on the run, the run, run, run, run! The presenter suddenly started screaming. RUN! They are coming for you! Suddenly, everything turned black and white and then vibrantly coloured like in those weird psychedelic '60s' and '70s' movies. The presenter's face swirling around and around warning him to run.

Act 3: 'Skinhead' Sam and 'Jihad' Joe

Trevor woke up in a sweat, ran to the bathroom and vomited.

***

Rain pelted down the alleyway, making a rat-at tat-tat noise upon the garbage bins. The police sirens illuminated the alleyway, the red and blue light gleaming off the puddles of water.

The neo-Nazi stared down the five policeman encroaching towards him. *How was he going to get out of this one,* he thought. He took a step backwards, nearly tripping over a garbage bag. The whole place was overflowing with trash; it followed the edges of the walls and piled up at the back, some in bins, some in black plastic bags and some just out bare. And if this wasn't bad enough, graffiti adorned the walls with such cheery remarks as 'We're all going to die' or an old classic, 'fuck you'. *This is what our country is becoming*, the neo-Nazi reflected, *absolute shit!* At times like these, it made him have great pride to be a skinhead, a soldier of Nazism (well, of the neo type); he was fighting to clean up his country so it wasn't all like this alleyway.

However, as much as he loved to think he was being very successful in his personal crusade against tolerance and all the other things a neo-Nazi hated, he knew he was really in the shit now. He thought back to his dead comrades, a tear rolling down his face. A tear he wiped away quickly; he wouldn't show weakness to the pigs. The fucking jihadists had attacked them, had come storming into the hangar, completely ambushed them, during their annual Hitler day celebrations. Though they'd given them a fight, they wouldn't take them out that easily. The police had been on the scene in minutes, but by then, it had already been a bloodbath. All were dead except for him and one of the jihadists. He ran one way, the jihadist the other. He briefly wondered whether the jihadist had escaped the cops. *Well, if he had, I'll get 'im*, he thought. He could hear the cops calling for him to put his hands on the ground. Like hell he would, he'd never surrender to the pigs. If this were to be his last stand, then so be it. He put his hand into his jacket, feeling the photo of his wife and…child. A momentary flicker of hesitation crossed his face, could he really leave her, especially after—but he had his duty, his mission. He pulled out the Uzi, wondering if this would be it, had the day finally come? If it had though, he would be sure to take at least a few of them with him.

"He's got a gun!" screamed one of the probationary constables.

The policemen pulled out their guns too slowly, only rookies they never had a chance. The neo-Nazi had already opened fire upon them. As they fell to the ground shredded by the power of the Uzi, they managed to get a couple of shots off at the neo-Nazi. One bullet hitting the neo-Nazi in the shoulder, another hitting him in the leg. As the neo-Nazi fell to his knees, he continued spraying the cops with bullets. Less than two seconds later, two thuds echoed throughout the alleyway, and then silence.

The neo-Nazi struggled to get up, wincing as his injured leg hurt even more from the effort. Blood gushed from the wounds, but he did not seem to notice. He looked around dazed, his vision blurred, his hearing almost non-existent. He looked up to the sky and screamed. He stumbled forward looking around crazily and noticed one of the policemen choking on his own blood. He shuffled towards the man and stood over him malevolently.

"Please, kill me," gurgled the man.

"Enjoy." The neo-Nazi grinned, kicking the man in the face.

"Ohh fuck!" the neo-Nazi screamed, as his legs buckled. Wasn't the smartest idea he'd had! By using his good leg to kick the man in the face, he'd put all the pressure on his bad leg, which could not handle it.

He pulled himself up, hobbled out of the alleyway and looked back once at the dying policeman, almost sorry for him. But that sympathy stopped at the almost, like the Muslims, pigs were just as culpable. As he pulled himself along the sidewalk, he saw police cars rush by, their whine, that sound! He'd heard it before.

The day had been great, the perfect day. A nice summer's day, cool breeze, yellow sun, blue sky, some lemonade for the kids, beers for the dads. Ah, the cricket on, drowned out by laughter and splashing from a pool. Clean cut grass, lush to touch, a BBQ cooking, the aroma of sausages and beef, salivating. Chats with friends not seen for a while, banter so good, even the old dad jokes seeming comedic gold.

Christmas music, Christmas kisses, of course, the day and the anticipation in children's eyes not gone. Parents plotting their Santa exploits for the night.

The sparkle of lights, clink of plates. The cool night's breeze. A day so great how could it get better. Tiring faces, still exuberant talk. Then the screech of tyres, shouts of men. Who could this be? We all get up…

***

The jihadist sat down on the train, looking around like a crazed dog for any sight of trouble. He'd run and not stopped running since the incident. He looked back on the incident fondly; his brothers were in paradise now and the infidels burning in Hell.

"We fucked them up good." The jihadist laughed.

"Oh my," gasped an old lady sitting across from him. His wet, dishevelled appearance disturbing her greatly.

"Raar," he roared at her, this provocation enough to send her flying towards the next carriage, probably the next two at that.

It took a long time after that for him to stop laughing, nothing made him happier than scaring infidels, well, besides killing them he reasoned. *Well, where was he to go now*, he thought. He'd have to leave Melbourne and quickly, probably Victoria too. They'd probably have already launched a manhunt for him. Bathing in a bit of pride for a second, he thought of his importance. He was a very good terrorist, probably most wanted in Australia. Thus, they'd probably be launching a manhunt in the adjacent states too, in NSW and South Australia, even Qld and Tazzie. Therefore, he knew the best place to go, where, in his mind, the words 'quality policing' had never been uttered. The Northern Territory, a place they'd never catch him in. But where would he stay, he thought. Well, it would be easy enough to steal an infidel's house, the place was practically abandoned he thought. He could probably even start his own terrorist cell there, Jihad Johns Terror Training academy, he thought. He knew it was a sin to show pride, like putting your name on your terrorist cell, but he knew Allah would forgive him for the small transgression. He noticed with interest a newspaper lying on the ground, it happened to be from the Northern Territory exactly where he was going. He briefly wondered how it had gotten there, but these queries dissipated quickly when he saw the ad on the front page. The ad read: 'Trevor's Fuel and Snacks, the only store for miles'. Perfect, Jihad John thought, it was almost as if Allah himself had placed the newspaper there for him. He pulled out his *Tafaha* (the Saudi rip-off of Apple) and searched up the store. Surely enough, the man was not lying, a rarity for an infidel. While he was on the 'sin box', he decided he may as well post on terrorbook the location of the store. *That's right, be confident*, he thought, *you will be just as good a terror cell leader as Mufasa.*

***

The neo-Nazi sat in the internet cafe, surfing the web for any mention of the incident and of a certain jihadist who escaped. He felt another tinge of pain in his arm, he'd have to get the bullet out soon, he thought. The only thing he had done to remedy his injuries was to wrap them in a bandage. As he read the latest ABC update, surely enough, the little bugger had escaped. He fumed as he read the article, which had several unsavoury remarks made about his neo-mates.

"Would you like a coffee?" asked a hipster waiter.

The neo-Nazi turned savagely towards the man, observing him scornfully. If he could even be considered a man, more like a little girl he thought observing the man's image. He saw his earrings, tattoos, man bun and hip clothes and came up with the ultimate reply.

"Coffee's for communists like you," he sneered.

"Wo, dude, chillax."

"I will once you fuck off," he rebutted.

The man ran off hurt, probably to cry (knowing these hipsters he thought). In reality, he was going out back to get his manager so that she could throw him out. Her reply was for him to suck it up and stop annoying the customers. Therefore, the hipster made the smart decision to ignore the neo-Nazi while at the same time making a concerted effort to give him dirty looks whenever he could. The neo-Nazi got back to his thoughts, trying to devise a plan to capture the jihadist. *You have to think like a terrorist to capture a terrorist,* he thought. So, he decided that the logical or illogical thing to do, if he was him, would be to post on terrorbook where you were going. All those Arab puffs loved doing that. So, he logged on, and surely enough, he saw the jihadists post, directing all fellow jihadists to follow him to the promised land of Trevor's Fuel and Snacks. Well, he wasn't a jihadist, but he was definitely going to follow the jihadist to the store, thought the neo-Nazi.

***

Trevor sat outside, staring at the wall. Now and then, he would casually throw a cricket ball against it, in the same spot as he always did.

"Oh, take it into the closet, you two." Trevor laughed, repeating the corny dad joke that always got him laughing. The origin of this exquisite joke coming from the fact that the cricket ball bouncing off the wall was leaving a red mark on it that looked conveniently a lot like a kiss mark.

As Trevor's laughs slowly dissipated, his face underwent a metamorphosis from amusement to stark reality. The reality that he was a depressed, lonely man not knowing what his place in the world was. Not knowing whether his life would ever not be a waste. He looked behind him at his makeshift cemetery; was it to be that his *only* impact on life would be to *end* others? He suddenly felt trapped, boxed in. All this ironic, as where in the world was it as open and bare as the outback? He turned around and saw with horror the bikie, who he had thought was dead, suddenly behind him. It all made sense to him at that moment, of course he couldn't have buried the biker, not in the state he was in. He must have never buried him, just pretended that he had, by piling back in the earth, with the grave half-finished, and placing a crude sign in front of it.

"Why'd you kill me?" said the biker hauntingly.

"No, don't worry I didn't, see it's all a misunderstanding. I didn't really kill you, so I didn't need to bury you either. I couldn't have buried you anyway! In my state, it would have been impossible. And look, you're right in front of me," replied Trevor.

"Why'd you kill me, what did I ever do wrong?" asked the bikie.

"Look, mate, you're not d—"

"WHY DID YOU KILL ME?" he screamed. "I'M DEAD, I…I…I'm dead." The bikie's screams slowly fainting away, as the fact that he had died, slowly seemed to dawn on his face.

"No, come on, you can't be. You're right in front of me."

At that moment, the bikie's flesh began to fall off, right in front of him, blood piling out everywhere, his whole body disintegrating.

"I'm d-d-dead," the bikie said, staring right at him for a moment.

"You did this," the bikie said half-heartedly struggling to walk towards him.

"No, it can't be." Trevor's brief moment of hope that the man, that he thought he had killed, was not actually dead, was shattered. He closed his eyes, praying for the sight to disappear, and when he reopened his eyes, it was gone.

***

"Mother-fucka!" screamed the neo-Nazi as he crashed his elbow into the window of the car that he was stealing.

After letting out a fountain of expletives, and picking bits of glass out of his elbow, he bandaged his arm and returned to the task of stealing the car. A car he had been lucky to find, as it was his favourite model. The car was the Ford Gran Torino 1972 Sport.

He put his arm through the window and fiddled with the door handle, opening it. He got in and relaxed in the leather seat. *Should probably get moving before the dickhead who owns this comes out and sees me*, he thought to himself. He saw to his delight that the car keys were in the ignition. He'd never wanted to damage the car more by hot-wiring it. What he had done already, by breaking the glass, amounted to sacrilege to him. The Gran Torino was a masterpiece that deserved reverence and respect.

He slammed the door shut, turned the ignition, and smashed his foot down on the accelerator, zooming off into the distance. As he was enjoying his experience in the Gran Torino, he suddenly remembered he hadn't checked in with his wife to tell her he was okay. She was going to kill him, he thought in fear. He slammed down hard on the brakes, sending his face into the steering wheel.

"Fuckity, fuck, fuck!" he cried.

He opened the mirror frantically and cried when he saw his nose, all broken and bleeding. He looked absolutely miserable, he thought. He turned his head rapidly to the left and laughed. *This is absolutely hilarious*, he thought, *this world*. He smiled and opened the door, leaving the car parked in the middle of the road. He looked forwards and saw the vibrant gleaming red cross of a pharmacy, a shining light through the darkness. He pushed the doors open theatrically and skipped in.

"Oh great, an Indian, I love Indians," said the neo-Nazi, observing the pharmacist's race.

"Can I help you, sir?" inquired the pharmacist.

"Yes, my good man, you fucking ca-an."

The pharmacist looked worriedly at the man; the neo-Nazi looked almost comical—bald tattooed head, bandages everywhere, and his beefy, tattooed and pale white body. He was like a parody of himself but a scary one at that.

"Okay, so what do you need?"

"A phone, bullets taken out of me and plenty of morphine."

The pharmacist looked up at the TV, back at the neo-Nazi. Back and forth four times, each time getting more and more worried.

"Listen, mate, we can do this the easy way or the hard way," said the neo-Nazi.

"Y-yes, I think I'll go for the easy way."

"Good choice, mate, you're not a fucking idiot."

"Yes, now let me just go and get the morphine," said the pharmacist walking straight for the backdoor.

"Oi! Stop! Stop now!" said the neo-Nazi.

The pharmacist bolted for the door.

"You bastard!" screamed the neo-Nazi scampering after him. The neo-Nazi jumped the counter and, just as the pharmacist was about to make it to the door, tackled him. The neo-Nazi winced as he felt the impact of the tackle on his leg.

"Now you listen here, you fuckwit, do you want to survive our little encounter?"

"Yes," said the pharmacist, quickly nodding.

"Well then, you better cut the funny business and help me right the fuck now. And hope to God, or whoever you Indians pray to, that you do a good job fixing me up," growled the neo-Nazi.

"Okay, sir, I can clean and fix you up in here," the pharmacist said leading him to the backroom.

"Sit on that lounge while I fetch supplies, sir."

"Fine, but if you run, there's nowhere you can hide, I will catch you. And about the phone…"

"Ahh, yes, sir, here use mine."

The pharmacist chucked him the phone and walked out of the room. The neo-Nazi dialled the number of his wife, turning the speaker mode on. He didn't trust the phones; they say they don't give you cancer when you put it up to your ears but that was obviously deep state bullshit. Suddenly, he heard the voice of a very angry woman.

"Who the fuck is this?"

"Hi, Martha."

"Sam, what the fuck have you been doing? I've been worried sick."

"Look, don't get angry, it's been hard, okay? Calling you has not been my first priority while I've been trying to escape the pigs."

"I know, but still…Damn you, Sam, you could have called. Running from the pigs is no fucking excuse."

"Sorry."

"Yeah, you better be. Are you okay?"

"Just a few flesh wounds, it's okay."

"Well, that's a relief. So did you kill all those pussies who killed our comrades?"

"Yes, I did, except for one."

"You fucked up there."

"I know, I'm going after him. I won't be back for a couple of weeks."

"The police know your identity, you moron! Don't come back here, the police are watching the house."

"Are you fucking kidding me, the ballz on those motherfuckas. I should come right over now and skin them."

"Don't worry, I have the boys on that." Martha laughed.

"Yeah, they'll make them wish they were never born."

"Look, I'll make a break for it and go to Tazzie, I'll stay with Bob. Once you're finished with the little worm, come there."

"Okay."

Martha hung up the phone on Sam. Then the pharmacist came in.

"Has anyone ever called you skinhead-Sam before, sir?" asked the pharmacist, making an attempt to be funny, a thing he did when he was very anxious.

"No," skinhead Sam said staring the pharmacist down.

"You get the joke though, as your name is Sam and you're a neo-Nazi." The pharmacist laughed awkwardly, wishing he'd never opened his mouth.

"Oh, hilarious. Well, I've got a joke for you. What do you call an Indian pharmacist who is really annoying?"

"I don't know," said the pharmacist, fear creeping onto his face.

"A rat," said Skinhead Sam getting up threateningly. "And do you know what you do with rats?"

"I don't know, sir. Please, sir, don't hurt me, I was only making a joke," said the pharmacist taking a step back.

"Well, I don't like jokes and I don't like Indians." Skinhead Sam moved closer to the pharmacist, a manic grin painting his face.

"So, what do you do with a rat punk, what the fuck do you do with a rat?"

"Please."

"You skin it."

"No, sir, look—"

"I'm about sick and tired of you, eavesdropping on my call to my wife. My wife, you scumbag."

"I didn't, sir."

"Then how did you know my fucking name, punk?" screamed Skinhead Sam, getting right into the pharmacist's face.

"It's on the news, it's on the news. It says, 'Sam Williams wanted for quintuple homicide' as the headline."

"Does it, does it? You wouldn't lie to me, would you, that would make me very angry."

"No, I wouldn't lie, sir."

"Well then, we're a-okay, mate." Skinhead Sam laughed, the tension in the room suddenly evaporating.

The pharmacist took a step back taking a deep breath. He'd remember this. Never make fun of a maniac, he thought, never again. And, he also thought to himself, it was probably a good idea to stop making jokes in tense situations, it always seemed to make things worse.

***

"Last stop, everyone please depart the train," said the conductor.

Jihad John got off the train; he'd have to drive the rest of the way to Trevor's store. He looked up at the stars, marvelling at Allah's creation. He'd always loved them as a kid. He'd even wanted to be an astronaut, but there was a much more important fight to be fought down here, he thought sadly to himself. *Maybe one day, when the war is won and the infidel menace is annihilated, I might find myself up there, if Allah wishes it*, he thought longingly.

He walked towards the parking lot and saw a man getting out of a yellow Peugeot 207. *Perfect*, he thought, picking up a large rock.

Jihad John walked behind the man who was busy inspecting something in the boot and smashed the rock into the man's head. He smashed the man's head in with animalistic ferocity, with no remorse at all. He didn't care if the man had had a family, even hoped the man would, so that he could create the greatest possible sorrow for an infidel. Blood patterned his body and face as he surveyed the dead body of the man, a smile beaming across his face. He looked for the man's keys in his coat. Finding them, he closed the boot and got into the car. He knew it was going to look suspicious, him being all bloody. But it was still night anyway, and if anyone tried to stop him, he'd kill them!

As he drove, he continued looking up at the stars, you couldn't see them in the city but out here! Allah, they were so beautiful. And so numerous, if only—he remembered as a child asking his father if he could go up there. "I wanna be an astronaut," he had said, but his father had scowled at him.

He had said, "They'll never let someone like you go up there." Of course, he had known about none of that back then. But when he'd started going to school, that's when he'd found out. Every day, he'd been called 'the Pakki Pussi', or 'Muhummad the Motherfucka'. He wasn't even Pakistani but Afghani! He'd told the teachers, but it had always just been a joke, 'boys will be boys' said the principal. But when it stopped being words and became physical, the answer still never changed. A blackened eye was just playful *banter*. But when he fought back, it was unacceptable *violence*. His hatred had grown and so had his interest in Islam. As his grades dropped, even in his beloved science, his hopes of going to the stars had faded away. But he had found a new glory, as Mufasa had shown him. There was a way to go to the stars, all he had to do was kill those who maligned him, who beat him, who destroyed him! Who destroyed his dreams! All he ever wanted to do was be in the stars, and for some reason, no one wanted him to do that. Why was it so damned hard for people to…he just wanted to be somewhere where no one would hate him, where he could just be in peace. Even his fellow brothers; they had laughed at his ambitions. Warned him about being sacrilegious; even they did not understand. Only Allah knew, but why did he not help him? Why did it seem he had forsaken him? But none of this mattered now, his dreams just fairy tales. The world was mean and harsh, and he had to be the toughest. He wanted blood, and he wanted everyone to feel what he felt. Desolation!

He glanced over at the ad for Trevor's highway store. He imagined the man as all those who had bullied him in the past. He had that kind of name, a jock's name, a dickhead's name. He remembered those dickheads and savoured the memory of killing some of them. He had turned up at their houses in the middle of the night, with a knife. He smiled, his teeth glinting evilly. He had made them pay. He remembered killing one. Stevo they'd called him at school. He'd played rugby, been all tough, but he wasn't so tough then. Especially when his knife had pierced Stevo's guts. He had done it slowly, looking into Stevo's eyes as he realised he was going to die. He'd pleaded, but just like his own pleas for mercy had fallen on deaf ears at school, so the same had happened here. The constant wedgies, punches, coming home bleeding. Now they would all pay. He'd come out of Stevo's room drenched in blood, red all over; he'd just kept on stabbing him, couldn't stop himself!

He remembered stabbing Stevo right through his stupid tattoo, the one with the viper. That reminded him, most of his bullies had been members of that gang, Viper Bikers. Those fuckers had all been so anti-Islam, inspired by some fucking martyr from the '80s. The only good thing the police had ever done was slaughtering that dickhead, shame they didn't kill the kid. The only thing that fuckhead got right was the anti-state thing. Those fuckheads had been the cause of his whole torment, of so many fellow brothers' torment. They'd always been radical, but when his brothers had found out an even more radical, solely racial gang had broken off from them (the skinheads), they knew they had to burn their scourge off the earth. But one of them had escaped, he'd get him one day. But maybe he didn't need to, years before they had killed his daughter, maybe they'd kill his wife next and let him live with the pain. Yes, that would serve him right.

***

The neo-Nazi looked into the distance; it had been a smooth drive. He was almost at the store now. He couldn't wait for the look of surprise on the bastard's face when he saw him there. That would of course be the last thing the fuckhead saw before he killed him. He pulled out the picture from his pocket and placed it on the dashboard. He had been happy then, so had his wife and his daughter. Mary, God, they'd...As he looked at his once attractive face, his hair! His clean clothes, his wife, even she'd changed so much since...They'd aged hundreds of years since that photo had been taken. As he looked in the mirror at himself now, his bald head, tattooed and unclean body and clothes, was it really worth it, after this? He was a monstrosity compared to who he was back then. A man living solely on a desire for vengeance. But he had to, he had to keep going. Even though it may irk his soul, no other father must experience what he experienced. Australia needed saving and he was the only one who could save it. Only he could cleanse the filth.

He'd made mistakes along the way, joined the Vipers who promised him revenge, bastard named Robbie had talked him into it. But they'd just been criminals, so he and a few likeminded guys had broken away and formed the skinheads. Following the words of the teacher, they knew what they had to do. He too had been wronged by the cops, by the state, by the half-breeds. So they had acted, taken arms. He knew he'd made a difference, made Australia a better place—or had he? Everything was still so fucked.

As he drove on and stared at the photo of his daughter, he couldn't help remembering the night. It had been the best day, the greatest day, but it had become a nightmare. He'd been living in a dream, but all dreams end. It had been just past nine. The sun had set, dessert had been served, the last drops of wine drunk. It was nearly time for the gathering to end. But then, they'd heard the screeching of car wheels. They hadn't thought much about it, some had remarked curiously on it but that had been all. He had been at the edge of the deck and had heard the sound of footsteps (dum, dum, dum, dum) and the click of AKs. He should have realised something was wrong, but he said nothing. It had been a great day, why ruin it? Why raise alarm, it was nothing. But it had been something. Then the shouting began in Arabic, they had run onto the deck, AKs blaring.

"If you move, we shoot," they had screamed, so they had all stood still, the children cried, the parents held them frantically.

The vicious eyes of the terrorist pierced each hostage, the sirens of police blared, the news roared.

'Twenty-three hostages taken in Australia's largest hostage incident in recent memory', 'Will they live?', 'How long will it go?', 'The nightmare before Christmas', even international news caught on, CNN, 'Tense hostage crisis in Melbourne's Suburbs', and BBC, 'Terrorists take hostages in Melbourne'.

The police arrived, ordered to do nothing, don't risk it. Talk them down they said, but everyone there knew by then there was no talking them down. You could see it in their jerky movements, their eyes, their speech. They just wanted an audience, and the police were all the more happy to let them have it. Moving in the news crews for filming, they were so preoccupied with them, that they didn't even set up snipers, in case...

Then, when the Channel 7 chopper was whirling up above them, they opened fire. They shot at the children first, he watched his daughter's friends disintegrating in front of his eyes. But that was okay, he was holding her in his arms. He would protect her...but he didn't. Neither did the cops who took too long to come, standing there like shocked hamsters. He should have turned his back to shelter her from the bullets, but he didn't. He was a coward. As the cops rushed in, he used...he used her as a *shield*. She was shot three times before the cops took down the terrorists. And he held her, bleeding in his arms. But the bastards wouldn't let him hold her. As his wife broke down in tears, and his brave face broke, they tore her out of his arms. They put her aside, waiting for an ambulance, which they…they had loaded their injured officers into first. His face was overcome with rage. One had only been shot in the arm, one a minor graze. Hardly mortal wounds! But they put them in those ambulances. And left his daughter alone to die. They were just as bad, their incompetence a mirror of the country's. On that day, he had seen the light, or rather the darkness. He had learnt it was time for a reckoning. And with that, he drove on, certain of his mission. Nothing and nobody would get in the way of it.

Act 4: The Meeting

From the deck, Trevor watched the approaching car. He wondered briefly who was in it. Regardless of the answer to that question, a sense of foreboding was attached to the car and the person in it. He shoved this feeling away. Stop thinking bad thoughts, think positive things, he told himself. But he knew that never worked, it only made things worse. That's all he was ever capable of doing. Making things fucking worse.

    He looked across the great emptiness as he sometimes called it. He felt kinship with it in a way. It was as empty and barren as his life. Seemingly purposeless, like his life, however unlike his life, it was beautiful. Unlike his life, it benefitted the animals that lived there, such as the kangaroo. Unlike his life, it was magnificent, with its brilliant red sand and iconic lush bushes that dotted the landscape. And most importantly, he thought to himself, it did really have a purpose. A thing that had eluded him his whole life. The only brief reprieve from this meaningless being when he was in the military and a young one. Or with Alicia. Alicia, it always came back to her, always to her. He could almost see her face right now, but his memory could never do justice to the pure beauty she was. Oh, what he would give to see her one more time, just one last time.

He cracked open his third beer for the day and by far not his last. As he began sipping it delicately, he returned to thoughts of the previous day. A day in which he'd killed again. The only witness, the outback. He wondered if God got a kick out of ruining his life. He wondered if God got a kick out of making him kill. He even wondered if he was really there. What God could do such terrible things, what God could turn a blind eye and let such terrible things happen. But no, he thought, as always blaming someone else. Blame God, blame the country, blame your dad or blame Robbie. It wasn't anyone's fault that his life had turned out like this. It wasn't anyone's fault but his. A serious moral deficiency, that was surely his problem. And his only solution to it, chronic self-loathing.

As he returned his thoughts to the incident, there was something he knew he had to remember. Something that was on the tip of his tongue, but he couldn't place right now. An occurrence that seemed to always plague you when there was something important you had to remember. *So, what was it, what was the damn fact he needed to know? C'mon think, brain,* he told himself, racking his brain over all that had occurred that day. And then, he remembered what he had been struggling to recall. The tattoo, yes, that was it, he thought. The viper and knife, Viper Bikers! A gang he knew well, his brother had been a member. The gang had done everything; robberies, extortion, smuggling, narcotics and murder. And Robbie had been at the centre of it all. Back then, he hadn't joined the Army yet, he'd still lived in Sydney. Ah, good old Blacktown, he reminisced about his old suburb, though he knew he couldn't fake it, most of his memories there had been bad. Well, at least the ones he remembered nowadays.

It had been tough for the two of them, his mother of Greek background had died at childbirth having him. Something that he had always blamed himself for, and something he believed his brother and father secretly did too. Their father was always in and out of prison. They'd had to fend for themselves, just two kids who had fallen through the cracks, all alone bar each other. In the early years, there were neighbours, the Robinsons, an elderly couple that had looked after them. They were the only real parents he'd had. But by the time Trevor was 12 and Robbie 13, they were dead. They'd been killed in a home invasion gone wrong, something that had enraged Robbie. He himself had just been saddened, overcome with grief. Robbie had screamed and shouted, swearing revenge. And one day, he did just that. He just came home with red splattered on his shirt and pants and ran to his room. He never talked about what had happened that day, but he remembered hearing on the news that the man suspected of murdering the elderly couple had been found dead in a gutter. His face mangled, broken bones everywhere. They said it would have been a very painful death. They said only some sicko would have done it. He had wondered if that was when Robbie had become involved with the Vipers. If he'd gone to them seeking answers and help, in exchange for loyalty.

Those had been bad days though, the early '90s, only a few years after Jessiah, that motherfuckin' cult leader, had been killed. He'd been quickly gaining a following and this only increased after his death. Crime, economic downturn and social unrest, the holy trinity, rocked the suburb and Australia. The Vipers were rising to be a massive force in those days—

drive by shootings every second week, mass murders, gangland wars. He would see it on the news each day, the special bulletin, 'Sydney Under Siege' with the ominous music. The reporter warned about the rising violent protests and strikes. Police going into these messes with black batons coming out with red ones. Even at night, he couldn't escape it, he'd hear the drone of helicopters, the chatter of gunfire. He'd flinch when he heard it, but there was no one to comfort him. Even the days began to become the night. It was everywhere. The sidewalks littered with dried blood, rubbish everywhere, homeless begging but no one with money to give. Gangs every next corner, ready to rob you if you weren't fast enough. The school pretty much barricaded, a permanent police presence, which didn't sit well with the school's criminal underbelly.

Trevor had always managed to stay out of all the crime and drugs, Robbie hadn't, it was as simple as that. Maybe it would have been different if the Robinsons hadn't died. But the signs had always been there. From the get go, Robbie had always been angry. He'd always been one of the bad boys. He'd been set on the criminal path, like their dad, from the get go. And nothing was going to change that. He knew he'd always been ignoring the signs; he should have done something. But then again, he'd had his own stuff to deal with. Self-centred as always, he reminisced. If only he'd thought about others for once in his life, maybe he could have made a difference. Maybe his life wouldn't be absolute horseshit. His life, it seemed, a torrent of what ifs. What if he had done that, what if he had acted differently, what if he had seen the signs? Any of these alternate scenarios preferable to the hell he lived in today.

They'd been the best of friends early on, Robbie and him, only a year apart. Playing backyard cricket and classic catches. Or the neighbourhood footy games, those games that often got a bit too rough. A broken nose, black eyes, scrapes and bruises. Only flesh wounds that they would all laugh away. Late nights drinking beers, listening to music and making out with his girlfriend Alicia. Back then, they were truly good times. Unreal times, but then, reality had had to rudely intrude again and take it all away.

Soon for Robbie, it hadn't been enough just having a beer, soon it had been cigarettes, then weed, crack and finally heroin. He'd like to tell himself it was just the Vipers being a bad influence that made him do it, but he knew that wasn't true. Trevor started to find stolen bikes and phones in the house, as Robbie's involvement with the gang escalated. When Trevor asked Robbie about it, he just told him to 'fuck off and mind his own business'. He should have acted then, called the police before it went any further. But he didn't and look what happened. Robbie dropped out of school at 16 and officially joined the Viper bikers straight away. He'd gotten that tat and everything. Though Trevor suspected he'd been a member much earlier, probably since that day he came home all bloodied. He'd heard rumours he'd been dealing at school, but he'd tried to ignore them; however, when he dropped out of high school, that façade was shattered.

His thoughts shifted back to Alicia. He remembered her silky buttermilk blonde hair. Her shiny blue eyes. Glossy red lips and fair white skin, unblemished by anything. Every element of her face delicately shaped, a pure testament to the Michelangelo God could be. He never knew why she had fallen for him, why she had loved him. She had said he was kind and that was enough. He remembered when he first met her, it had been year three. He remembered being captivated by her beauty and elegance. She had seen him staring and came over to him. They had talked. He had cracked corny jokes; jokes he had memorised to entertain his brother, and she had laughed at them. Something that had been far and apart for his brother. Even from that first moment, puberty still four years away, he knew he had loved her. First, they had been friends, then lovers. Always faithful and always truthful. He remembered when she had first entered puberty, those awkward looks she had given him. Waiting for him to experience it too. And then he did, and then things were great.

He remembered the night clearly; he didn't know when, but at some point Robbie had started dealing heroin to Alicia. He didn't recognise it at first, if only he had earlier and tried to stop her, maybe things would have gone differently. As usual, he had been waiting outside her house, ready to pick her up. But she wasn't coming down. The minutes kept ticking by and she hadn't come down. Something was wrong, he had felt it. The minutes just kept ticking by, why wasn't she coming down? He didn't know how he knew, but he knew she was gone. He had walked gravely down the path to her home. He had opened the door and walked towards her room. And there she had been. Lying dead on the floor. Another young victim of heroin. The moment he saw her dead, he knew he would never love again.

A tear rolled down Trevor's face; he looked out, the car was nearly here now. He saw the car gliding across the asphalt. And he saw himself running wildly towards his home, his great despair had turned into great rage. It had been Robbie's fault, he had given her the drugs, he had killed her.

To this day, he wondered if she really had been dead yet; he had fled the scene like a coward, afraid to answer the questions of her parents, to face an imagined wrath that would befall him. He wondered whether, if he had just called the ambulance she might have been saved.

He had rushed into the house, slamming the door shut.

"What the fuck are you doing here, you shouldn't be here now!" screamed Robbie covered in blood.

"Why are you all bloody?" whimpered Trevor, all the rage dissipating, replaced by the horror of the sight he saw before him.

He remembered it had been like a bad nightmare; however, the nightmare never ended.

"What are you doing here, you shouldn't be fucking here."

"Is that your blood?" he remembered asking, but when he saw the look on Robbie's face, he knew it wasn't.

"Get the fuck out!" screamed Robbie.

"You've changed! You used to be my brother, you used to be a good person and now you're just a killer. I can't believe you…" They both stood there in silence for a moment not knowing what to say next.

"You know, she's dead," Trevor said at last.

"Who?"

"Alicia, you motherfucka, you killed her with your fucking drugs," cried Trevor accusingly, remembering his rage.

"My god, I—"

"You killed her, you're just a fuckup like Dad, you know that. A fucking failure."

"Oh, you're fucking talking, wadda 'bout you? You're no fucking hero, what are you?" said Robbie walking up to Trevor and shoving him, a tear rolling down his face.

Trevor never said another thing to Robbie; he remembered his uncontrollable manic rage. He just kept beating Robbie up, punching him and yet Robbie did not lay a fist on him. At some point, Trevor had pushed Robbie into the next-door room, and that's when he saw the bodies. They were those of two men, two dead men. Blood was everywhere.

"I'm sorry," said Robbie.

Trevor had run out of the house and not stopped running until he had been picked up by a police cruiser. He had told the cop everything and they had arrested Robbie after that. He remembered the moment, the police lights illuminating the darkness. He saw his brother's face, betrayal splayed across it. He had joined the Army soon after that, looking for a purpose which he briefly found. That being killing. He had believed it would be great fun, an adventure, a paradise compared to back home. Ironically, despite joining the Army to get away from it all, before he ended up like Robbie, the Army just messed him up more. And like Robbie, all that had happened is that he had come back from the Army a killer too.

How had it happened though, he wondered. When did all the violence in his life start? He knew that it crept in before he joined the military with everything that went on. But when did he become a killer? When he joined the military? Was it when he killed for the first time in combat? Was it his tenth confirmed kill, his twentieth? Or was it when he stood by and watched two members of his platoon kill an innocent villager. Something that he would never forgive himself for doing.

Was it his punishment for letting it occur, that his men would all die the following day? A question so unsettling, he wished he'd never thought of it, though it was a question so ever present in his mind. He should have done something, but he hadn't.

He looked up and saw the car had now reached his store. He took a large gulp of his beer and chucked the can over the side of the deck. He got up, shaking the stiffness out of his legs. He watched as the man got out of his car, holding in a laugh as he did. Goddammit! The man looked comical. He looks just like a neo-Nazi, Trevor thought to himself. The big beefy figure, bald head but, *goddammit*, he thought to himself now chuckling, *he's been in the wars*. The man was bandaged in multiple places. The bandaging done in an almost farcical manner. He noticed the man's car and whistled; he'd always loved cars, and as any car lover will tell you, if you love cars, you gotta love the Gran Torino. He loved his HSV, but the Torino was something else entirely.

"Wanna beer, you look like you need one!" shouted out Trevor.

"You bet!" shouted back Skinhead Sam coming towards him.

"On the house." Trevor laughed chucking one to the man, who caught it.

"Thanks, mate."

"Love your car."

"Thanks, I love it too."

Skinhead Sam walked up onto the deck sitting next to Trevor; he couldn't see the jihadist anywhere. But he'd be here soon, and when he arrived, he'd be waiting.

"So, what brings you to this part of the world, and more specifically, to my store?" asked Trevor.

"Waiting for somebody."

"Really, who?"

"None of your biz, mate," said Skinhead Sam, laughing the question off.

"Well, anyway I'm glad for the company even if you're not buying anything," said Trevor meaning it.

"Must get lonely, being out here all alone."

"That was the original point. Name's Trevor, by the way; what about you?"

"Sam."

The two men shook hands.

"Has anyone ever told you a good nickname for you would be Skinhead Sam?" Trevor laughed.

"No, no one has ever told me that." Skinhead Sam squeezed his hands, anger rising in him. He didn't like people making fun of him. Trevor, ignorant of the rising tension, continued on.

"Yeah, everyone had a nickname back in the Army, it's a habit for me nowadays; I often give people nicknames without even realising it."

The tension was released as Skinhead Sam looked at Trevor with admiration. He always had great respect for soldiers who fought for their country; he wished everyone was a great patriot like them.

"You served?"

"Yes, siree, Afghanistan three tours, one in Iraq."

"Well, thank you for your service, mate. I wish every man served their country admirably like you."

"Yeah, well…" Trevor looked out into the distance; he wouldn't wish armed service on anyone. Not after what he'd seen and done. The two of them sat in silence for a while, drinking beers.

"How's West Ham doing in the Premier League, haven't got any internet here. Don't tell me they've been relegated." Trevor laughed.

"Wouldn't know."

"Oh, you don't follow it?"

"Why would I, they are all niggers that play in it. Not one fucking white man in the Premier League."

"Whoa, man. Bit racist there," said Trevor, taken aback by the harshness of the man's words. So eager for human interaction, it dawned on him that the person who was speaking to him right now might indeed be a skinhead.

"What! Don't fucking tell me you're one of those snowflake pricks." Skinhead Sam was taken aback by Trevor's defence of those sub-humans, the people who killed his daughter. How could a man like himself, who served his nation, do such a thing?

"I'm no snowflake, mate (*I'd melt in this outback heat if I was*, thought Trevor laughing inside his own head for a second at his own wit), but that kind of talk's not okay."

"C'mon, are you serious, a man can't even use the 'n word' today. Well, guess what, nigger, nigger, nigger, nigga, whadda you think about that!" screamed Skinhead Sam, getting increasingly angrier.

"What do you even have against black people, mate?"

"What do I FUCKING have against them, well, don't even get me started. Them and their Muslim and Asian buddies are destroying this country." *This man didn't understand what he was fighting for,* he thought, *just another ungrateful sod who protected those who wished to kill him.*

"Who are you waiting for?" asked Trevor cautiously, for the first time worried about who might be coming, who this man could be waiting for.

"A dead fucking man."

Shit, Trevor thought, he'd gotten himself into trouble again, *first a bikie and now a neo-Nazi. This was becoming an unpleasant trend.* Whoever this man wanted to kill, he couldn't let him kill him. Or at least not here. He couldn't take another confrontation, not now. And what did he owe to this nameless 'dead fucking man'? For all he knew, the man could be just as unsavoury as the one sitting next to him right now. He just wanted peace! Did that make him bad or selfish? Did not wanting to feel like a piece of shit for just one day in his life…

"Look whatever business you have, just carry it out somewhere fucking else," said Trevor getting up.

"No, I won't. You're fucking lucky you served or you'd be dead already, Trevor! Now, what's going to happen, is I'm going to conduct my business, and you're going to go into your store and stay there all quiet." He wouldn't let anyone get in the way of his retribution, especially not a traitor like this man.

"You know I can't do that."

"No, I fucking don't," said Skinhead Sam getting up; deep inside, he hoped Trevor would give this up, because if he didn't, he'd have to kill him. But even though it might be unsavoury, he had to do it, for the good of the nation, for his daughter.

"Look, asshole, just leave, please just leave."

"Well, you asked for it." Skinhead Sam smiled, although inside, his inner turmoil raged, he would be tough, merciless now.

Skinhead Sam launched himself at Trevor; Trevor ducked the attack and ran for the door. The man was twice his size, he knew he couldn't beat him one-on-one, but maybe he could find something in the store to level the playing field. He looked behind as he dashed for the door, the man was getting up again looking even angrier than before. He opened the door remembering the rifle he kept behind the counter on the wall. It was an antique, but he hoped it would still work. He jumped over the counter and pulled the rifle off the wall. If he remembered correctly, there was one bullet inside it, that would be all he needed. He looked in front of him and saw the man coming towards him. He saw him in his sights and aimed. However, he made one mistake, he hesitated; he didn't want to kill the man; he did not want to kill again. Skinhead Sam did not hesitate and in that moment jumped over the counter and tackled Trevor. For a minute, the two men grappled with each other, turning over and over, neither man having the advantage over the other. Skinhead Sam thrust a left hook into Trevor's face, fazing him for a second, a second that he used to grab the gun. Skinhead Sam got up and leered over at Trevor.

"It's over."

"Please," pleaded Trevor putting his hands in front of his face, as though his hands could stop a bullet.

"Bye, bye." Skinhead Sam laughed maliciously, the man had gotten in his way and gotten what he deserved.

Trevor heard the explosion of the gun going off, but he realised seconds later he was still alive. How could it be, was he a ghost? He heard a loud thud and removed his hands from his face.

The gun had backfired!

Trevor turned away; he couldn't look at the sight. The man's face was absolutely pulverised. Trevor got up shell-shocked by the explosion. For that reason, Trevor did not hear or notice the yellow Peugeot arrive at his store. And for that reason, he didn't hear the footsteps of Jihad John as he approached the store. And for that reason, he did not hear the door open and the bell chime. When Trevor turned around, he saw the jihadist all bloody, standing there right before him. All he could say in response to this occurrence was this: "Fucking hell, another one."

"Thanks for taking him out for me." Jihad John smiled, crusted blood adorning his face.

Trevor gave up, he'd had enough for one day, for a whole lifetime. So he decided the best course of action was to faint and ignore the reality that faced him.

Sometime later, Trevor woke up dazed, taking in his surroundings. He noticed he was tied to the counter and struggled to get loose, but to no avail. After retiring from this line of action, he took the time to wonder why he was still alive. The man in question was obviously a killer, hence the blood. And from the glimpse of the man's visage that he had gotten, the few seconds before he had fainted, he had noticed that the man had that dangerous look about him. And, as though the jihadist had read his mind, he walked in and delivered him an answer.

"If you're wondering why you're still alive, it's because of a little hobby of mine."

"And what is that?" asked Trevor, fearful of the answer that was coming.

"Torture. A truly joyous passion of mine, oh, what a wonderful thing it is! But what method shall I use with you today? Psychological, no, physical I think. Maybe a classic such as waterboarding or the nail pulling. Maybe even an old goodie, Soviet if I remember right, hooking you up to a car battery. Would you have wires for that?"

"Ah, yes, in the car section, Aisle 4." Trevor couldn't believe himself, saying this, was this Stockholm syndrome?

"You know it really helps when the person getting tortured helps; it makes it all the better experience," said Jihad John going over and collecting the wires.

"You know you don't have to do this," pleaded Trevor.

"Oh yes, I do." Jihad John smiled, walking over to get the wires.

Jihad John thought to himself that Allah had not really said anything about torturing the infidels, just cleansing the world of them. But he was sure he wouldn't object; what would he care for the wellbeing of the unholy? And anyways, it was so much fun, watching the agony and fear on the faces of his victims. Serves them right for following a false god, he thought to himself, serves them right for ruining his life. All those bastards deserved to suffer and be punished just like he was.

"Why, why are you fucking doing this?" pleaded Trevor with anguish.

"Well, for what else, other than the glory of Allah. It is my mission to purge this world of all infidels."

"That's ridiculous! So you're one of those fucking terrorists I hear about on the news!"

"Only the best."

"Well, please, you can just let me go, no one will need to know about this. You don't need to kill me, your god, Allah, would not want that to happen."

"Do not say his name, infidel scum!" screamed Jihad John, slapping Trevor in the face.

"Please, please, just…" pleaded Trevor to no avail.

"I show no mercy to Western materialist scum." *They never showed mercy to me*, he thought to himself. He was the monster they had created; it was people like Trevor's own fault for their own reckoning.

Trevor gave up on trying to plead for mercy from Jihad John and went on the offensive.

"Well, guess what, fucka, I've met a few of your mates in Afghanistan and Iraq, and let's just say I said hello to them with some of my friends. Y'know, bullets," taunted Trevor violently.

"I'm going to enjoy killing you slowly, infidel. Day after day, you shall ask for death and will not have it. And then finally, when I'm bored of you, I shall feed you to the wolves. Not that there will be much left of you to feed to them."

Trevor stared the jihadist down, not letting him see the intimidation he was feeling.

"You know what," said Jihad John dropping the wires, "I think we'll start with waterboarding today."

The jihadist crouched down to Trevor's face and knocked him out with a savage punch.

Trevor awoke yet again finding himself tied against the tap's piping. He tried desperately to remember his military training to survive torture. However, most of it relied on staying alive long enough for the SAS to save him. And the

SAS wasn't coming this time. Trevor struggled vainly to try and escape, pulling desperately against the piping. He wished he was as strong as he was in his heyday—then he might have been able to escape—but unfortunately, he wasn't. Jihad John came back inside the bathroom and slowly filled a plastic jug with water. The jihadist watched in delight as the terror increasingly grew on Trevor's face.

The jihadist finished filling up the jug and walked vitriolically towards him. Jihad John put the rag over Trevor's face, which Trevor tried to resist futilely. He moved his head violently from side to side and bit out with his mouth. The jihadist then proceeded to slowly pour water on it. Trevor struggled to breathe as the water filled his lungs. The pure pain was unimaginable, an intense burning that didn't seem to be ending, ever. As Trevor struggled desperately, the jihadist just continued pouring the water on the rag. His lungs were on fire, filling up with water. Just as Trevor felt like he could not survive the pain anymore, it stopped, and the jihadist lifted the rag. Trevor lurched forwards coughing up water, desperately gasping for air. The intake of air only seemed to fuel the flames of pain in his lungs.

"Did you enjoy that?" asked the jihadist with an evil glint in his eyes.

All Trevor could do in reply was cough.

"You know, it's rude not to answer a man when he's talking to you. I guess I'm going to have to teach you some manners."

The jihadist got up and closed the door.

"Please, no…not again," cried Trevor desperately trying to get the words out of his mouth.

The jihadist laughed maniacally.

From outside the door, the strangled screams of Trevor could be heard, interspersed with the sounds of gurgling, choking and the pouring of water. As the torture continued, Trevor began to grasp the eternal punishment that would await him in Hell. For the first time in his life, he was petrified, if he died…He had to live, and, in some sense, find redemption or else. As each waterboard passed by, Trevor's chest heaved forwards, he screamed, cried, yelped, but no one came, nor did mercy. Drool ran down his face, but it did not stop. He could barely breathe, but it did not stop. The pain overwhelmed him, but it did not stop.

Hours later, the jihadist came out of the room smiling; it was night now.

Time flies when you're having fun, Jihad John thought. He'd exhausted waterboarding now, he'd start with the nails later tonight and then lashes next, he thought. But he needed a break, torture really took it out of you. He hoped the man wouldn't die; he'd barely made it through the last few waterboardings. He had much more fun planned for him and didn't need him dying on him now. He needed a drink, a heavy one, he thought. He knew Allah forbade it, but he was doing his work now; he was sure he could be given an exception. It's not like he did it too often. As he indulged himself more in thoughts of what liquors he could have, he came to the conclusion that a nice spirit would go down quite well. He'd have to ask the infidel where they were. Jihad John walked over to Trevor's body and kicked him.

"Where are the spirits, infidel?"

"Spiritss…?" said Trevor delirious.

"Yeah, alcohol, you know."

Luckily for Trevor, in his delirious state of mind, he had a stroke of genius which he did not realise. Unluckily for the jihadist, it didn't end well for him.

"In...tha carr sexshion, metho iz a branndy iya recomend."

The jihadist walked over to the car section and found the bottle in question. So eager for a drink, he did not even think twice about the location of the drink. In the darkness, he did not notice the warning sign which read, 'Poisonous. Do not drink. Ingestion may cause death!' Jihad John chugged the bottle, so quickly he did not notice how it tasted funny.

That was a really bad spirit, thought the jihadist after he finished drinking it. Minutes later, his vision started blurring, then he couldn't stand upright, then he dropped down to the floor frothing from the mouth. Then he died.

Act 5: Moonlight Reveries

Trevor woke up and struggled to his feet, he'd been left untied. Where was the jihadist, he thought to himself, fear instantly creeping back into his heart. He looked out into the rest of the store, the moonlight illuminating the room. Then he saw him, splayed across the floor. Was he dead, drunk or asleep, wondered Trevor. He couldn't be dead or could he, wondered Trevor. Trevor went to one of the aisles picking out a hunting knife and came over to the jihadist, getting ready to fight him if he was not dead. Trevor noticed the empty bottle of Metho by his body and suddenly laughed; he had drunk methylated spirits thinking it was alcohol. Well, he was surely dead then, thought Trevor kicking the jihadist. When the jihadist did not move, Trevor bent down to check if he was breathing. When Trevor was satisfied he was not, he moved over to the deck, but not before getting a few beers from the fridge, and by a few that meant six cans.

Trevor relaxed on the folding chair, gazing out into the distance. There was a certain dreamlike quality to the experience, the absolute stillness of everything. He wondered briefly if he was dreaming. Maybe he was, maybe he wasn't. But he didn't really care to find out the answer to the question, because finally it was peaceful, something that had eluded him for the past couple of days.

No, he thought to himself looking back over the past day, he wasn't sorry that those two bastards were dead. He wondered defeatedly to himself, whether this was his purpose in life, to purge the world of scumbags. He'd come here to get away from it all, yet trouble seemed to follow him everywhere. Would he ever get peace? Probably not, he observed cynically.

As the minutes passed, beers were downed. As the hours clicked by, Trevor found it increasingly difficult to work out whether he was awake or dreaming. He could see the asphalt slowly morph into a river of blood, the bodies of all he had killed directly or indirectly floating in there. As he looked in horror, the river slowly moved towards him. Soon it had engulfed the whole store. The blood surrounded his body, but he couldn't scream or move, which only made it so much worse. The river carried the store along; every now and then, the moonlight would illuminate the face of one of those he had killed. Some faces smashed up, others unscathed. He saw the bikie's face, then his own brother's, but he wasn't dead, or was he? He saw those of his platoon, he saw Private Smith's perfectly intact as the last time he saw him, disintegrate as the darkness rolled over him. He saw the villager that had been killed by his men. He could have saved him, like so many other faces in this river of death, but he hadn't.

Suddenly, the river dissipated leaving the store perched over a cliff, he looked in horror as a giant viper began to push the store over the edge. But it wasn't only a viper anymore.

No, it was everyone he had ever killed, everyone whose death he had caused and those that he couldn't save.

Soon he was falling, falling through to hell. A place he knew he belonged. A place he knew it was inevitable he was going to visit one day. A visit that would never ever end. He was going to die, he thought to himself. It's all over. *And maybe that's what I want,* he thought to himself.

Trevor lurched out of his chair, feeling his body and looking around for a second, making sure that he was still alive. It was just a dream, he thought relieved. He turned back and looked at the store, seeing the jihadist's body was still there, and of course, the purée that was Skinhead Sam's head. Trevor knew he had to leave the store; he couldn't go back to sleep here; there were too many ghosts. He went into the store, picked out a sleeping bag off the shelf and a few beers. As he walked out, he briefly glanced at the corpse of the neo-Nazi, or as he had called him, 'Skinhead Sam'.

"What a waste!" he exclaimed.

How many others like him had thrown their lives away in the service of the devil? Whether he masqueraded as ISIS or a Nazi, he lured men to their deaths, in service of a fake cause.

He walked out into the distance, as if in a trance. Downing beer after beer as he made his journey to nowhere. He felt the sand beneath his feet massaging him towards slumber. He looked up at the sky, the stars shining brightly. He goggled in amazement at their splendour; he could see the Southern Cross and even the Milky Way. He wondered yet again if he was dreaming. A breeze gently blew against him; he inhaled the sweet cold air. He listened to the mesmerising lullaby of the cicadas and the other musical instruments of the outback, like a baby coddling him to slumber.

Trevor heard a gentle rustling from his left, breaking him from his trance. He instantly turned to see what it was. In the bush, he noticed two eyes staring at him.

"Whoever it is, you betta come out," he said slurring his words.

There was no response, making Trevor all the more nervous. He looked again at the spot where he had seen the eyes, yet there was nothing there anymore. He decided to continue walking and ignore the occurrence. Every now and then, he would notice those eyes again, he wondered who they belonged to. He hoped not a dingo. He'd heard stories about dingoes, and they weren't all that nice.

He thought about the past day's events and wondered whether he would ever be able to go back to the store. He wasn't sure if he would be able to. Not after what had happened there. It was time to start moving again, 'cause evil had found him yet again. The moon was covered by clouds and soon all he could see was darkness everywhere. He ruminated over his lack of foresight to bring a torch, but he wasn't going to stop now, he knew he had to get as far away as he could from the store. He wondered whether he would be able to outrun his ghosts this time. He knew he wouldn't be able to. As Trevor continued his nonsensical journey, it was abruptly ended by his tripping over a stray bush and being knocked out.

He dreamed he was at the SCG, it was India v Australia. It was Steve Waugh's last test; he was 80 not out. The crowd was ecstatic; it was going to be a fairy tale ending to the man's illustrious career, surely he was going to get the century. Then Trevor had the greatest idea in history—wasn't that what everyone who had had a bad idea in history had thought? He ran over to the fence and jumped it. Tearing off his clothes as he ran buck-naked towards the pitch, but for some reason, the game wasn't stopping. Steve was distracted by the sight, and as he turned to stare at the spectacle, he was bowled. His stumps went flying. The crowd was hysterical; they were blaming Trevor for getting Steve out. They were blaming him for ruining their lives. When he looked at Steve's upset face, he realised it wasn't Steve Waugh's face anymore but the face of everyone he had let down. So many faces, so many dead.

"You should have done better. Just following orders going into that village, we all knew it was bad," said Private Smith.

"I..." muttered Trevor.

"Why didn't you call the ambulance?" asked Alicia.

"How come you got to come home?" questioned Lance Corporal Wilson.

As the voices began to multiply, Trevor found himself unable to withstand it anymore. He began to keel over, trying to block his ears, but it only got louder. Trevor looked up at the sky and was blinded. He covered his eyes and huddled into a ball, beginning to rock back and forth like a baby. But the voices only multiplied. He felt hands touching him, pulling him, scratching him. Trying to pull him into the dirt.

He awoke to find it was daylight now and that there was a dingo staring directly at him. This time, he screamed in real-life, causing the dingo to flee. This was followed by projectile vomiting. Trevor struggled backwards frantically, hoping the dingo would not return, but soon enough, it did.

"I know Brazilian jiu-jitsu," Trevor threatened making Bruce Lee-like gestures.

"Ruff!" barked the dingo.

"Oh, so you know taekwondo, do you?"

"Ruff, ruff," replied the dingo.

"A blackbelt, eh, well, guess what, I'm a rainbow belt. I'm so good that they needed to create a new belt just for me. Beat that punk!"

"Ruff!"

"Not impressed, well…" At that moment, Trevor realised he had just been having a conversation with a dingo. Was he really that messed up?

"Guess I had a bit too much to drink, mate," stated Trevor, settling back down to go to sleep, forgetting the presence of the dingo. He reasoned it must just be a figment of his imagination.

Trevor was awoken moments later by the sound of intense licking. Trevor slowly turned his head to the side. He observed with disgust that the dingo was licking up his vomit. *So he was real*, he thought.

"That's nasty," remarked Trevor watching the dingo lick up the vomit.

"C'mon, stop it. Off it!" shouted Trevor, shooing the dingo away. The dingo turned and growled at Trevor, then returned to licking it up. By now, he had become accustomed to the dingo's presence and was not afraid of it anymore. It didn't seem to want to eat him, so he'd let him do what he wanted to do, and in return, the dingo would let him do what he wanted to do.

Trevor got up, picked up his stuff and began to walk away. He heard whining and looked behind him, seeing the dingo sitting on its hind legs. *Well, that's a bit odd,* he thought.

"Are you my little shadow who's been following me around?" asked Trevor.

"Ruff," said the dingo, giving Trevor cute eyes.

"Well, all right, mate, C'mon. I could use the company, even if you're just a dog," he called out cheerily, patting his leg.

The dingo came bounding towards him, only slightly offended that he'd been called a dog.

"I shall call you Bob," said Trevor addressing the dingo.

Bob looked up at Trevor, his eyes gleaming happily.

"Well, come on, Bob," Trevor called as he began to walk back to the highway store, wherever it was.

As Trevor trudged forwards, every minute, every second, dehydration set in. The sun beating down on his face, his skin burning. Even his Mediterranean skin could not withstand the intensity of the sun. As his lips parched and his stomach rumbled, he became increasingly desperate to find the store. He didn't want to die out here, becoming increasingly pessimistic about his chances of survival. Of all the places and all the things in the world, it couldn't be the outback that would do him in. But as with everything in his life, it wouldn't go the way he had wanted it to, so why should death be any different? At this point, he didn't even know if he was going in the right direction. Trevor looked forwards; all he could see was the endless desert. He saw crows circling above him, eager for a feed. Their black bodies contrasting the bright blue sky. *Not yet*, he thought to himself. *You won't be getting a feed today.*

Trevor kept on walking into the distance. His vision becoming hazy, his bones struggling to hold up his body. In desperation, Trevor imagined he could see the highway store getting very close. And not long after that, he managed to convince himself it was right in front of him. Trevor ran desperately towards it; Bob ran eagerly after him. He was nearly there, just one more step, just one more step, one more…

Every time he got close to it, it got further away and soon it just disappeared. Trevor collapsed in misery; it was over, he thought to himself. Trevor looked miserably over at Bob and remarked sadly that it was the end for him, and that Bob should run away and save himself. He lay back and decided to die quietly. Seconds later, Bob was sitting on him licking his face.

"Goddammit, can't I even die peacefully?" shouted Trevor.

Bob moved back whimpering.

"I'm sorry, Bob," Trevor said, instantly regretting his outburst of anger, his voice so croaky his words were barely legible.

Bob came towards him; he saw in his eyes that he wanted Trevor to go on. He knew he couldn't let down another person, even though Bob wasn't a person, just a dingo.

Trevor struggled upwards; well, if he couldn't die peacefully, he'd just have to die struggling. He moved forwards slowly, every now and then almost falling. If he would have fallen, he was sure he never would have gotten up again. His skin became a reddish brown, the sunburn causing him to itch uncontrollably, yet he continued on through the pain. His pants were torn, his shirt torn in half, his hair scuffed, and sand seemed to cover every inch of his body. He was by now completely delirious, his vision blurred, his speech inaudible. He kept on rambling and slurring out the names of people, especially the name Alicia. Bob continued to trot after him loyally. He was wondering to himself why it was becoming increasingly hard to stay awake. He daydreamed of water to refresh his parched mouth, imagined the cool refreshing feeling as it trickled into his mouth. He imagined its soft, silky texture. He imagined the sound of it dripping and gushing.

He imagined a drip-drop, drip-drop, drip-drop. But he wasn't imagining it anymore, he had stumbled onto someone's farm, and in front of him was a tap that had been left partially on. Trevor ran to it crazily. He stuck his mouth around the tap gulping mouthful after mouthful of water down.

Bob nudged him, giving him an annoyed look.

"Oh, sorry about that mate, here you go," croaked Trevor, allowing Bob to have a drink.

Trevor looked over and saw a tree that provided a nice bit of shade and decided it would be an ideal place to rest. Trevor slouched down and felt his sanity and awareness drain back into him. He watched Bob sleeping happily in front of him. *What a wonderful dingo*, he thought to himself. It occurred to him that it was odd that the dingo was so good with him, it seemed almost domesticated. This thought haunted him for some reason, though he couldn't place it. As he looked at the dingo, he felt guilty. Why should such a beautiful creature be given to him? There were so many others who were so much more deserving. As he mulled over this thought, he slowly drifted off to sleep, a welcome reprieve from consciousness, though he knew he would dream and, in those dreams, he would be trapped, unable to escape the unimaginable horror of his past.

***

The Chevrolet Suburban's windows were shattered by bullet holes. Bullet holes that adorned the whole exterior of the car. The man opened the door and got out, feeling his head. His jet-black hair stood out, in contrast to his pale white skin. His bright red mouth, to his shiny pearl white teeth. His solid chiselled jaw, to his plump cheeks. His clean-shaven body without a speck of hair, to his female-like bowl haircut. He donned a black jacket and dark grey jeans, but if that was not enough to tell you this man was a killer, you only had to look at the eyes, black as charcoal. He tried to remember the shootout, but it was all a blur; at some point, he must have been knocked out. He'd been instructed to take the drugs and the money by his employers, but somehow, they had known. When he and three of his men had driven up, they had been shot at. Though unfortunately for them, they weren't the best shots, whereas his men were professionals. That hadn't stopped them from taking out everyone but him though. He looked around him, seeing bodies splayed everywhere. A grin slowly appeared over his face, oh, how death got him off. As so often occurred, he was the lone survivor. Then he saw a man to his left resting against a ute, breathing heavily. A bullet to the guts had got him. He walked over to the man slowly and pulled out his gun.

"Please don't."

He crouched down to the man holding the gun out to his face.

"You wouldn't have perchance seen where my dingo ran off to?" he asked.

"I saw him go west. Please, don't kill me, I have a son, I'm all he's got," said the man.

He let the man pull out his wallet to show him a picture of his son.

"See my son, please."

"Maybe I might pay him a visit," snarled the man.

"No, please."

He shot the man in the head twice, instantly feeling the predatory elation of a kill rush through his veins. Now he was the lone survivor, he smiled again at this thought. His mouth widening even more than could be thought humanly possible.

The man walked over to the only car undamaged and got in, his pet dingo had run off and he was going to find him. He only loved two things in his life, Santa's Little Killer (the dingo's name) and killing people. And he wouldn't let anything get in the way of those two things. He had run west so that was the way he drove.

Every now and then, the man would get out of the car to observe the dingo's tracks, which he had somehow found. His hunter instincts beaming with the chance to track his prey. Soon he noticed a man's tracks had joined those of the dingo's.

"So, someone's tried to take me dingo, well, well," said the man in his deep, crackly voice.

He would kill whoever had taken his dingo, and he would enjoy it. He looked forwards into the distance with steely determination. Once he committed to something, nothing got in his way. Like how he'd committed to killing all those years ago. He'd been introduced to it by Jessiah, who all those years ago had revealed to him the fun of killing. And oh, how right he had been. He had told him, as a young child, kill! Kill them all! And he had graciously accepted, chaos the man had said, he wanted chaos! And he had been very happy to deliver—

he'd killed his parents first, an experiment that lit his passion. His father had bashed him and laughed, well, who was laughing then, he smiled. He caressed his arms for a second, the image of a beast had been replaced by that of a scared child. For only a second, he was not man but boy again, hoping Father would not come home drunk again. He returned to beast again, remembering his next steps in his metamorphosis. He had next begun picking people at random, just sitting at the train station and staring. Those he picked he'd follow and…well, it wasn't the greatest of days for them; he licked his lips savouring the memories of his kills. But of course, he needed money, so he'd joined the Vipers enterprise. Getting paid for killing, he had thought, was practically a scam. The more ruthless and violent he was, the more he was paid. Ahh, it was heaven, they said if you loved your job, well…

Act 6: The Hitman

Trevor awoke to see a farmer standing over him. The farmer was in his early 70s, his hair still retaining a greyish tinge. His face was sun damaged, red and friendly. The farmer was skinny as a stick but could move well considering his age and frame.

"You all right, mate?" asked the farmer.

"Ahh, yes, I'm all right, bit hungry though."

"Well, we can fix that. What exactly brought you out here, bit out of the way this place is?"

"I know it'll make me sound like a real galah, but I got lost. Just walked out into the desert, trying to get away from it all. You know what I mean."

"I know what you mean, mate. I see you served then."

"How'd you know?"

"I served too, Nam."

The two men stood there in silence for a moment. Both remembering the trauma of their service.

"Well, lucky you found the place, you could have died out there."

"Yeah, I know."

"What about him?" said the farmer pointing to Bob.

"That's Bob, found him, well, more like he found me. Wouldn't leave my side."

Bob got up at the mention of his name looking the farmer up and down.

"Crikey! Dingoes are savage beasts down 'ere. I once heard a story 'bout a baby, taken by a dingo and eaten. They're not usually friendly characters; to keep one of those, you have to be a crazy bastard."

"I know what you mean, seems almost domesticated, not at all wild."

"If I were you, I'd be worried about the owner of that. I don't know one friendly character who'd own one of those."

"Well, now you do." Trevor laughed.

"We'll see, mate, you did break into my property and steal my drink. Bloody drought and all."

"Sorry 'bout that."

"Well, anyways come on, let's get going. Wife'd kill me if I was late for dinna."

"Sure, and thanks for everything."

"No need to say anything, it's the Aussie thing to do, helping a mate in need."

"You should tell the Melbourners that," said Trevor jokingly.

"Ahh, a Sydneysider," said the farmer laughing.

"How'd you know?"

"Everyone knows about the bloody rivalry, it's not a top secret! Anyways, they're not all as bad as you Sydneysiders try to make out, wife's a Melbournian."

Trevor beckoned Bob to follow him, which Bob obeyed eagerly.

"He can sit in the back of the ute," said the farmer opening the Toyota Hilux's boot.

"Okay, Bob, come here," beckoned Trevor patting the back tray of the ute.

Bob jumped into the tonneau and the farmer closed it up.

"He'll be fine back there?" questioned Trevor.

"Don't worry, I put my dog back there all the time."

Trevor and the farmer got into the car and began the drive up to the house.

"How far is the trip?"

"Couple of k's."

"Wow, big farm you have here. Anyways, how'd you meet your wife, last time I checked Melbourne's a long way away from the territory."

"Wait for dinna, she tells the story betta then me."

"Will do."

The two of them sat in silence for a couple of minutes until the farmer broke the silence, searching for conversation.

"You been watching any of the sports, lately?"

"Nah, don't have TV or Wi-Fi."

"Wow, how do you live without it?"

"Sometimes I ask myself the same question. Anyways, I enjoy being disconnected."

"You probably don't even know who won the election."

"Don't worry, someone already told me about Scomo. I own a highway store, people that come by are my only source of news, so I do find stuff out. Though I must admit business has been slow recently, so my current affairs aren't that great." Trevor shuddered remembering the events of the last week.

"I'm sorry to hear 'bout that."

"Me too, anyways do you know who won this season's BBL? I'm a Thunder man myself, how'd they do?"

"Not too well, I'm afraid. They came sixth."

"Damn, who won?"

"The Renegades, it was a Melbourne-Melbourne final," said the farmer laughing.

"It couldn't be worse," said Trevor jokingly.

"Guess they've got this one over you guys, mate."

"Well, there's always next season, mate, you watch."

"I will. You know, if you're so patriotic about Sydney, why'd you leave?"

"I had to get away from it all," replied Trevor distantly, repeating the same vague term as before.

"Are you going to elaborate or…" The farmer ended his interrogation of Trevor when he noticed the look on his face, the look of hurt. He knew that look too.

"Don't worry, no need to say anymore, but know if you want someone to talk to, I'm here," said the farmer understandingly.

The two of them sat in silence, remembering their pasts. Trevor stared out the window, watching the scenery go past.

"Does it ever go away, the hurt?" asked Trevor solemnly.

"Some days," replied the farmer.

They arrived at the farmhouse to find the farmer's wife waiting for them.

"Who's that?" questioned the farmer's wife.

"Found him at the fence, says he got lost in the desert," replied the farmer.

"Really?" The farmer's wife laughed.

"'Fraid so," replied Trevor.

"Well, come on in then you two, dinner's on the table. I'm sure there's enough there for you."

"Where can Bob stay?" questioned Trevor.

"Who?"

"Ah, sorry, Bob's the name of the dingo."

"Right, well, he can sit out front with Marcy; I'll make sure to bring him out some food."

The dog and the dingo galloped towards each other, eager to sniff each other's butts.

"Marcy can always sense a good one, real strange dingo you have, mate," said the farmer's wife.

"Tell me about it."

Trevor wolfed down the bangers and mash.

"You're really hungry, aren't you?" said the farmer's wife.

"Tends to happen when you haven't eaten for a day. It's good, by the way."

"Thank you," replied the farmer's wife.

"So, how'd you two meet, your husband told me you tell the story the best. Oh my god, I can't believe it. I haven't even properly introduced myself yet, we don't even know each other's names. I'm Trevor."

"Well, I'm Melinda and my husband's Clive."

"Well, nice to meet you, Melinda and Clive," said Trevor.

"So, you wanted to know how we met, well, it was the summer of '71, Clive had just returned from Nam. Back then, Clive was an absolute mess."

"Luckily for some reason, she saw something in me," interjected the farmer.

"That I did, I first saw him in a bar in Melbourne. He'd literally just got off the plane and was already drunk. My first thought when I saw him was that he was an absolute drongo, but then, he got to talking to me. He was a real charmer back then and a looker. Convinced me, he did, that I was a bit tense and needed a massage. Best one I've ever had."

"Still to this day, I reckon she just married me for the massages," said the farmer.

"Oh, stop it. Anyways, you know, things went on from there; we stayed up laughing all night; I know it sounds corny, but it's true."

"That wasn't the only thing we were doing," said the farmer naughtily.

"Oi, you, I'm the one telling the story. Anyways, well, he told me he was going back to the family farm in the territory in the morning and asked me to come. You know, I could see the pain in his eyes and knew I just had to do it, plus it may have helped that I knew right then and there that I loved him."

"And we've lived happily ever after since that day," said the farmer.

"I've gotta say you have quite a story; it's just like it's right out of a film," said Trevor.

"Well, thankfully, the film had a happy ending." The farmer's wife smiled.

"Well, I wish my story would have a happy ending," remarked Trevor sadly.

"I'm sure you'll find someone," said the farmer's wife sympathetically.

"I did," said Trevor looking downwards.

Trevor looked up at the ceiling, wondering what he would dream of tonight. What grotesque, foreboding nightmare would plague his sleep. The farmer had agreed to drive him to the store in the morning; he was thankful for the man and his wife. They were really good people, not just in action but truly caring. He reminisced about his sadness at the mention of his lost love and how the farmer's wife had intuitively tried to make him laugh to relieve the sadness. Yes, they'd all had a few beers, laughed and truly he had felt happy for the first time in a long time. He wished he could give them something special, but what could he give them? A cheap highway store present, a fishing rod. Maybe he'd go back to Alice Springs and get them something special. He found himself purposefully trying to avoid thinking of the store. But such is life, whenever you try to not think of something, you think of it. *Not tonight please*, Trevor pleaded with his inner psyche, a constant war he was always losing. *Oh please, God, just one time, please just let me rest, let my past rest, let the world rest.*

And for once, he did.

Trevor woke up, showered and dressed. He stared at himself in the mirror; he had become a ghost, he thought. He walked down the stairs and sat down for breakfast, enduring casual talk. Who should be picked for the ashes squad? Or rugby union v league, which was better? Some of the more notable topics of discussion. After this, Trevor and the farmer walked outside to the ute for the long trip home. Trevor beckoned Bob, who looked longingly back at Marcy before trotting up to Trevor.

"Okay, mate, in here," said Trevor pointing to the tonneau, Bob obliged.

"Well, shall we?" questioned Trevor.

"Guess so," replied the farmer.

They both got in, exchanging goodbyes with the farmer's wife before heading off.

As the ute drove through the desert, it left a flurry of red dust in its wake. It was as if the ute was a paintbrush and the desert its canvas, painting strokes of red elegantly across it. Trevor looked out the window, wondering how long it would be until he was back.

***

The hitman saw the farm's gates and smiled.

"Well, well," snarled the hitman, seeing the tyre tracks.

The hitman jumped the fence and began the long walk to the farmhouse. He'd soon have the dingo back, he thought happily. As he took the long walk to the farmhouse, he wondered how he'd kill the fools. *Quickly, slowly, quickly, slowly. Enjoy it,* he thought to himself. But he knew he wouldn't be able to resist the urge to kill straightaway. Though when he was able to, it was ever so sweet.

***

The farmer hopped out of the ute and up the stairs. *That man, what was his name, oh, yes, Trevor*, he thought. *Nice bloke but teetering on a knife's edge*, well, he remembered what that was like. He hoped he'd sought out his problems, though he knew from experience that was easier said than done. It always seems in this world, the good sleep bad and the bad easy, he remarked to himself. Well, maybe that would change one day he hoped. Though he wasn't too confident about Trevor's chances. He'd seen the same look in that man's eyes as in the eyes of soldiers in Nam. Those had been the eyes of broken men. Some came home broken shells of a man, but most with a broken neck or a bullet in the head. He wished that he could have helped him more, but he himself wasn't exactly in the best state either. *Well, such is life*, he thought to himself not knowing that Trevor had uttered the same words the night before.

That's odd, he thought, as he walked up the stairs. Marcy usually came up to meet him when he came home, but where was she? And god, it was too silent. He remembered that silence. Somehow there was a death silence, back in the Army, all those silent villages. Whether it had been them or Viet-Cong, it didn't matter, they always seemed to leave villages empty and silent. He wanted to call out her name, but something held him back, something was wrong. He'd learnt the instinct in the war, or maybe he'd always had it. He crept up the stairs, as much as his elderly frame would allow. The door was ajar. Melinda never left it open. She would never have left it open 'cause she didn't want the mozzies and flies getting in, let alone a wild dingo. He slipped into the house and crept towards the dining room. His training kicking in. *Where'd I keep the rifle*, he thought to himself, jogging his memory. *It wasn't the same these days, was it? Well, that's getting older for you*, he remarked internally. Oh god, he was a massive fool, right on the wall, that's where his trusty Winchester was. He entered the room and walked straight to the wall, not noticing the two shapes, one face down on the table, the other standing there watching. He took the rifle off the wall, loading the cartridge hanging next to it. As he fiddled with it, pushing ammunition in, he finally noticed the two shapes.

Oh god, he thought, *oh no, please not you.* His fingers shook, he couldn't lose her, no, no!

"Where is he?" asked the hitman.

"I'll kill you," the farmer whimpered.

Jostling even harder with the rifle, he couldn't understand how this had happened. Who was this animal, who had rudely intruded into his life and shattered it into a thousand pieces? He became even more anxious as he saw the man lift his pistol, he knew he wasn't fast enough, not anymore. The hitman fired one round straight into the farmer's head, blowing his brains out the back of his skull.

Well, the hitman thought, *the bastard wasn't here. Obviously*. Maybe he shouldn't have killed him so quickly, he should have taken more time and had fun. But no one, no one at all, insults him like that and lives a second more. But how was he going to find the man now? *Well*, he guessed, *I'll just have to kill everyone in the territory until I find him*; he laughed grossly. As he walked out the back door, he trampled the remains of Marcy; he never cared for dogs, they were weak, domesticated shrimps who weren't worthy of sharing their lineage with true killers such as wolves and dingoes.

Act 7: Alice Springs

Trevor walked out of the highway store, now happily intoxicated, and looked over at the burial yard. Two new graves now adorned it. Both had similarly distasteful signs labelling them. The first read: 'Skinhead Sam, died a bastard, died a fool, now a Bonehead Sam'. The second read: 'Jihad John, reckon you'd get on well with Satan, similar hobbies. Maybe he can show you some of his skills in a practical on you'. He laughed manically at both of these signs. He reckoned his signs were getting better now. Soon he reckoned he'd be writing whole stand-up comedy pieces on the graves. Trevor suddenly felt a lightbulb go off in his head. A genius idea unrivalled by the greatest scientific minds' discoveries. He should go on a drive to Alice Springs. It was probably double demerits today too, so if he got pulled over, he'd be given a ticket.

"Why not?" he screamed, which seemed like a perfectly reasonable idea.

In his drunken state, he began to imagine an audience of fiends were watching his every action. He was there for human entertainment, and it was a dramedy. He looked up at the sun as though it was a camera and did a little twirl. He was sure as hell going to put a show on for the bastards, he thought, skipping theatrically towards the HSV. In a glimmer of clarity, he saw through the facade his drunken state was creating. But he dismissed this, he had to get away from the store anyway. And what good was reality anyway?

The HSV zoomed away, swerving from side to side (frankly embarrassing as the road was smooth and straight). A bird landed on the porch of the store and Bob watched it, instantly distracted from wondering where his human had run off to. Bob watched the bird walk into the store, his eyes widened. *Yes*, he thought to himself nonchalantly, *I do feel like a bite to eat.* So Bob followed the bird in; he hadn't been inside the store yet, he observed. As he trotted into the store, his fickle mind was yet again sidetracked by wondering whether there was food anywhere in the store. Completely ignoring the bird now, the dingo began exploring the store for the first time, his little nose sniffing furiously as he snooped around. He walked over to the bloodstain on the floor and sniffed it, investigating. He wondered briefly what had happened there. He trotted around the counter also seeing similar stains and bits of brains. For some reason, he suddenly felt disturbed by these things and decided to bark a couple of times to try and alert his human that something was wrong. However, he soon forgot this feeling as he noticed the bird again. He chased after it eagerly, but every time he would get close, it would just flutter away. After a while, Bob gave up and walked away, downtrodden, to the porch, sitting down beside Trevor's chair. He felt like a nap, after that he would go and find some food.

Trevor drove into town, thanking God for the miracle that he was still alive, his drunken state having evaporated. He didn't know how, in his condition, he had managed to make it into town alive and uninjured, but it had happened. Trevor had glimpses of what had occurred on the trip, but nothing really flowed properly. He remembered driving through bushes and having genius ideas such as taking a cross-country route. He also remembered that manic laugh that seemed to emanate from him throughout the journey. Whether it was the drink that made him do it or a masquerade he had put on to hide his inner strife, he did not know.

Trevor got out of the car and began walking down the main street. He didn't know where he was going or what he was doing, but he just had to walk. So that was what he did, until he reached the end of the street and then decided, what the hell, why don't I walk back the other way. Once he reached the other side, he decided it was prudent to walk back the other way again. People gave him curious yet scathing looks as he walked up and down, but Trevor took no notice. Unbeknownst to him, two men stood there watching him with eager eyes.

"He's mine," said Father Callaghan.

"No, he's mine to save; we all know I am more skilled at saving the lost than you," replied the Greek Orthodox priest named Yiannis.

"I saw him first, God wants me, not you, to save him."

"Oh, don't you dare, you pretender, charlatan, fake, idolater! You know full well myself and my church's teachings are the correct ones, unlike yours."

"Oh please, Yiannis, we all know full well you're just a sour old fool who just disagrees with me to disagree with me. And anyways, a fool as you are, you'd have no chance of saving him."

"So?"

"So?"

"Why don't we have a little challenge then, you *vlakas*, we both try to save him and whichever one succeeds can admit to the other that he is the better Christian."

"Ahhh, very tempting. A full-on battle, Catholic v Orthodox—who will come out on top? Who will be superior? Yes, I will play this little game, obviously it won't be hard, but I shall win."

"Keep dreaming."

With that, the two priests went off, each concocting a plan to 'save' Trevor.

Trevor wondered to himself how many times he had walked up and down the street. Probably ten, maybe twenty. Well, he wasn't counting, and it didn't really matter, he would continue doing this till the pain stopped, although he could do with a beer, a cold frothy brew. Trevor decided he'd had enough of walking up and down the street and decided to walk into the newsagents; he was curious to see what was happening in the world. *Nothing good*, he thought to himself, *nothing good at all is probably going on. Shit,* he thought to himself, as he searched his pockets for cash, both of which were bare. Well, he could always have a sneaky look at the papers. That never hurt anybody.

Trevor walked in and walked out quickly. He had seen the front cover of the Territory Tribune and it was all he could do to hold in a well of tears. It read, 'Husband and Wife Killed in Brutal Murder'. Underneath it, it had their photos. And Trevor knew those faces. Oh god, he knew those faces. The faces of the farmer and wife who had helped him. Melinda and Clive. But it wasn't just their faces, it was Alicia's, Smith's, Stewart's, Robbie's, the villagers. *God, why did the good only die*, he thought to himself. Trevor didn't know why they'd died, but he knew it was his fault. Everyone he cared about, anyone who was good to him seemed to die because of him. And this would be no exception. He looked around him, people were staring, he had crawled into a ball and was rocking on the ground crying. It had finally caught up with him; he couldn't drink or hide it away forever. He tried to get up, but every time he attempted to, he just fell back down, as if getting pulled into the ground by all those he had let down.

"Why God, why!" he screamed, looking up into the sky, into the heavens. His stare accusatory, his face contorted in anguish.

Now as he looked around himself, it seemed he was in the middle of the road, was this his subconscious telling him it was time? Time to give up, time to give in to the darkest of desires. Death! He could hear yelling or at least he thought he could. People telling him not to do it. What now, yes, this was it. He felt the cold steel of a gun in his hand and raised it to his head. Where had the gun come from, he did not know. Where was he now, well, he didn't care. It would all be over soon.

"Stop it, my son," said Father Callaghan running, as quickly as his elderly frame could take him, to Trevor's side.

Trevor didn't know why he stopped, but as he loved an Irish accent, which the man displayed heavily, he decided he'd stop and listen. He could always shoot himself later, he thought bitterly.

"Come, come. You need to rest. Come with me, my child, it'll be okay," said Father Callaghan, helping Trevor up and walking him towards the cathedral. Trevor looked up at the spire as he entered, wondering if God had finally intervened in his life to help him. No, that was the wrong way to put it, he *hoped* God had finally intervened. But hope never seemed to get him anywhere in his life.

They walked inside, the priest sitting Trevor in a pew, while he brought up a chair.

"Let it all out, my child, let it all out," he said as Trevor continued to cry. Callaghan gently patted his back, soothing him as he let years of tears out.

"What's wrong, my son, what causes such deep sadness in you?" Callaghan questioned.

"I've done terrible things, horrid things. I…I don't have a purpose. I don't have a *life*. I don't have anyone!" Trevor cried in increasing ferocity and desperation.

"Come, my son, come, confess," Callaghan said, leading Trevor to the confession box.

Trevor walked in, wondering if by some miracle he would be saved, if he even *could* be saved or *deserved* to be saved at this point.

"Confess, my son, confess your sins and you shall be absolved."

So Trevor did He confessed about the murders he had committed and the deaths he had failed to stop. He confessed that he had betrayed his own brother, his own blood, and that he had failed the men he led into battle. He confessed that he did not always believe. He confessed that he did not stop the murder of the villager and that he broke the commandments frequently. 'Thou shalt not kill' being broken with liberty. Even though he had pledged not to kill after he'd gotten back from the war, he had killed. Even though he had pledged no more violence, violence had come and found him. *Violence, his dog, man's best friend*, he thought sarcastically, *always coming back to find him no matter where he ran off to.* However, for some reason this time as he admitted these things out loud, he didn't feel bad, he felt rejuvenated. Like some bad poison was being sucked out of his body. And when he finally finished and was absolved, he knew, well, he didn't quite know what he knew, but he knew it was a start, on the road to redemption.

As he walked out of the box though, he accidentally immediately sinned yet again when he let out a…

"Who the fuck is this?" Trevor screamed jumping back in fright when he saw Yiannis.

"You," said Father Callaghan with distaste, noticing Yiannis.

"Oh, ahh, sorry for the curse, Father."

"You are absolved," said Callaghan lazily.

"My turn! Doesn't look fully saved to me yet. Oh, and I heard everything so no need to repeat it, mate," said Yiannis, the Orthodox priest.

Yiannis led a bewildered Trevor towards the Orthodox cathedral opposite the Catholic one. Trevor looked back at the Catholic one now, noticing how odd it was that there were two cathedrals, both very grand, opposite each other in such a small town. It almost seemed to Trevor as if the two were competing. No, Trevor thought when he saw the billboard on the Orthodox cathedral; it *looked* very much like they were competing. The notice read, 'Catholics burn in Hell! If you don't want that to happen to you, join the Alice Springs Orthodox Church!'

Well, that's pleasant, Trevor thought to himself, noticing yet another unsavoury sign adorning the Catholic Cathedral.

Yet again, Trevor was sat down in a pew, and yet again, a priest pulled up a chair.

"Do I sense some Greek in you?" questioned Yiannis.

"Certainly," replied Trevor.

"Well, are you Orthodox?" questioned Yiannis.

"Kind of, kind of not. Generally, just Christian if you know what I mean."

"Ahh, yes, I do, well, you are a good Greek boy, yes. You know, before we get onto you, what do you think of this new poster I made, it sure should put that Irish son of a bitch in his place."

"Erh."

"Oh, sorry, I sometimes accidentally swear; I get carried away, please forgive me, God," Yiannis appealed.

Trevor took a look at the poster and laughed. It was almost comical what seemed to be going on in this town. The poster was of Jesus on the cross and it read, 'The Romans killed Jesus. The Catholics are traditionally known as Roman Catholics. Coincidence? I think not'.

"You like it?" questioned Yiannis.

"Well…"

"Of course, you do. Anyway, onto you. I heard your confession to Father Callaghan, sure he treats you like a baby. Waves away your sins, great. But I tell you, I tell you the truth. You're being a little *malakas*. Okay? You get sad that you killed a twat, well, a couple of them. When really, I think, that is your purpose. Right, those three guys were bastards, and well, if I'm not mistaken, maybe it was God who preordained that you should purge this world of those guys. Now don't get me wrong, I'm not saying you should be overjoyed at their deaths, I'm not saying you should seek out death. But the way

I see it, if death seeks you out, you end it. If you know what I'm saying. You gotta stop shying away from the fight and killing yourself over it and start facing it and stopping it. Look, you beat yourself up, blame yourself for things you had nothing to do with. And look, you blame yourself as being uncaring, of being selfish but think about it. You obviously care, you're obviously not selfish, look how much you're berating yourself over your mistakes."

The more Yiannis talked, the more Trevor knew what he had to do. He knew what he had done was wrong, yet it was also right. A paradox, like life. Nothing was black or white but *grey* and it'd just taken him a while to realise that. He'd been forgiven for his sins; he knew they'd still haunt him, but he also knew that it wouldn't be as bad. *At some point in your life,* Trevor thought to himself, *you just gotta forgive yourself and move on. The past is the past and you just gotta move on to the future, lest you find yourself trapped in it.* He thought philosophically briefly, wondering what had driven him to this realisation. Was it an accumulation of grief and reality, the experiences he had endured? Or one random thought, a thought to forgive himself. A thought that instantaneously sprouted and grew and caused a change. Well, he didn't think he'd ever really know, but what he did know is that the two priests certainly helped.

"So, do you understand?" questioned Yiannis.

"Yes, I do. And I've gotta just say thank you. Thank you, thank Callaghan, thank this town and God and life. Look, I know you're not going to like this, but I'll say it anyway. You two, Callaghan, Yiannis. Quite the team. Maybe if I could heal, maybe you two could too, just saying." Trevor winked at the end.

And without another word, Trevor walked out. He had brought a tear to Yiannis' eye, but he'd never know that. He knew he would avenge the deaths of the farmer and his wife; he didn't know where or when, but seeing as things were going so far, he'd probably turn up at the store. He turned as if to go to the bar for a quick drink but thought better of it. It was time to start facing reality, not escaping it.

As Trevor walked away, the two priests came together.

"Who won?" one of them asked, not really caring for the answer anymore.

The other replied simply that Trevor had won. Although Trevor himself had done nothing explicitly, he had inspired the two men. A Catholic and an Orthodox coming together to help a man, maybe there was hope that the schism in the town would end. Because if a broken man could heal, maybe they could too.

Act 8: Facing the Darkness

The hitman walked towards the highway store smiling. He knew this was the place, something had drawn him towards it. He laughed inside himself. It almost seemed as though an unseen puppeteer had been drawing him along this path, the past few days, he thought to himself. Odd...The hitman got closer to the store and noticed a Camry parked in front of the store. *Could this really be the man who'd stolen his dingo? A man who drove a Camry, let alone a 2008 model!* He'd expected more of a man who stole another man's dingo. *Well*, he thought sadistically, *it didn't matter what they drove, their brains still had the same colour when he blew them out.* This again caused him to smile. He remembered he'd often been called the smiling assassin, because ending human life always brought elation to him. Not just joy but elation, something deeper, not just a superficial little thing like joy. When he killed, he felt truly satisfied.

***

Jerry Jones was up from Adelaide and particularly angry today. His big fat jolly face now red and scowling. The aircon in the Camry had died, followed by him having to change a spare tyre in the scorching heat. And if that was not bad enough, he bitched to the dingo, he had run out of food. The dingo looked up at the man's waist which protruded like the titanic as it sank. He tried to see the man's face, who stood crouching over patting him, but it was blocked by his meteorite.

"And," continued Jerry, "if that was not bad enough, I just ran out of food and water. Luckily, I found this place, but as today's luck would have it, of course the proprietor is nowhere to be seen."

"Ruff," barked Bob as if to say, 'why don't you just take stuff and run, it's not every day you get a freebie'.

But of course, Jerry would never do that as he was an upstanding (even though it was sometimes hard with his portage) citizen who had a manic obsession with following the rules.

"I guess I'll have to just wait here, bloody cockup this whole thing's been. From day one, I swear. Never should have gone on this bloody trip. But you know Melissa from work, my rival in accounting, said she'd done a trip from Adda to Alice. She showed all the pics and was like, 'oh my, it was so enlightening and spiritual.' Y'know, all that bull. So then, of course, I had to outdo her, and I was like, 'Well, guess what' (in a real gruff voice right) 'I'm driving from Adda to Darwin.' You should have seen her face; she was absolutely fuming. Of course, I had to do it now, I'd opened my stupid mouth. Every day she'd ask, right in front of everyone, mind you. 'When you going to do it (in her stupid high-pitched bogan voice, right)?' So eventually, I broke and said tomorrow, which I can assure you my supervisor wasn't too happy about…"

As Jerry continued talking drivel, he was oblivious to the man coming towards the store. Bob was not. He remembered the distinct smell of the bad man. And he knew there was trouble, a-coming. Bob vainly attempted to alert the man to the danger by barking tersely, but the arrogant son-of-a-bitch just continued on with his ramblings, assuming the dingo was just showing his appreciation for his 'genius' storytelling skills.

The hitman walked up the stairs, pulling out his pistol. He saw the shape of a very fat man through the window. *Seriously, it could not be this fool*, he thought to himself. Something inside him, was it his gut? Yes, it was his gut, his gut was telling him it was not this guy, but he was certain that this was the place. He thought about it a bit more and realised it wasn't his gut telling him this, it seemed to be something more spiritual, even though he didn't believe in that shit.

He pushed the door open cautiously and walked in. He moved his gun from side to side, canvassing the area to see how many targets there were. When he was sure it was only the very fat man, he sighed in disappointment. He had been hoping for at least three victims today.

The hitman heard the now incessant barking of the dingo. *So, this was definitely the place*, he thought. The fat man had now seemingly sensed the other man's presence, as he turned around. His facial features morphed from that gossipy face that people get when they're telling a story about themselves, while seemingly taking a dig at people they hate, to utter surprise.

"Hey, what are you doing?" asked the unfortunate patron at the store, his eyes staring at the gun.

Bob slowly back-walked, he knew what was about to happen and knew it was time to get out of Dodge.

The hitman slammed his gun onto the counter.

Jerry, also sensing the danger, made an attempt to run at the door, but the hitman simply pulled up his gun and pointed it at him, shaking his head.

"No, no, no. No running, the fun's only just begun." He laughed maniacally.

Jerry slowly walked backwards, frightened. Bob was now cowering behind the counter, completely forgotten by the hitman, who was so engrossed with the quarry in front of him that he had forgotten his primary objective.

"No, no, don't be afraid a…what is your name?" teased the hitman in a voice that was supposed to be soothing but just came off as creepy.

"J-J-Jerry," Jerry replied petrified; as he spoke, pee came rushing down the sides of his legs.

"Well, *Jerry* (he said with emphasis on the Jerry), you're not so talkative now, ha, ha, ha, ha, ha," he laughed with increasing insanity.

Jerry continued to creep backwards as the hitman only moved closer, scraping his gun along the counter as he did so.

"Y'know, *Jerry*, I don't usually do this, but I'm feeling groovy today. You a gambling man, *Jerry*? You sure are gambling with diabetes I see." He laughed yet again.

The only reply the hitman got from Jerry was a frightened little side glance.

"Well, *Jerry*, I love to play the pokies, but nothing gets me off more than the real hardcore shit. You know what I mean?"

Silence.

"C'mon, *Jerry*, liven up a bit. I'm talkin' about the good shit. The Russian roulette, the coin flip of death. But I gotta say two up, that's a favourite of mine. More like two down if your number's called." The hitman laughed at this last remark of his, his deep, crackling voice echoing throughout the store.

He pulled from his jacket a well-polished, wooden two up stick. With two 20-cent coins delicately poised in each circular hole. He ran his hands over the stick, caressing it lovingly.

"So, here's the deal, *Jerry*," the hitman said tapping the gun gently on the counter, "you win, you get to leave, you lose, well, *Jerry*, I wouldn't want to be you. YOU GET IT!" The hitman screamed the last part.

"Y-yes," said Jerry nervously.

"You know the rules?"

"Yes," said Jerry more confidently now.

The hitman could see the confidence and hope seeping back into the man. That's what he liked. His favourite part of this was snatching that away.

"So, *Jerry*, what'll it be…"

"Obverse."

"Reverse."

"Or you feeling real lucky…"

"Ewan."

Jerry looked intently at the stick and called Ewan. The hitman grinned and flipped the stick. The coins landed on the floor, and for what felt like an eternity, they rattled from side to side until they stopped.

"Heads and tail, my man, you are lucky," said the hitman; he could see the joy in the man's face. He could almost taste the hope, the hope that emanated off him. He licked his lips savouring the taste.

"So I can leave then?" asked Jerry cautiously.

"No, *Jerry*, you can't leave. Well, not in the way you mean. But of course, I've gotta oblige by my words. I said if you won, you could leave. I'm not a cheat or a bad sport, really I'm quite honest. So, *Jerry*, of course, you can leave. Just not in the way you mean. Maybe that's not fair, but it's truthful. It's truthful to life, let me ask you this, *Jerry*, is life fair? You just go on, abiding by all the rules. Living out your life in peace and har-mone-ey, never do a wrong, always pay the bills. Then you meet someone like me, *Jerry*. Just in the wrong place, at the wrong fucking time. So, no, *Jerry*, life's not fair, so why should this game be? But having said all that, yes, *Jerry*, I'll let you leave. Just not in the way you intended."

***

Trevor got out of the HSV Maloo, looking from side to side. Time seemed to freeze for him. He saw his boots slowly hitting the ground, picking up orange dust. He saw the sweat beads drip down his face. He saw the highway store standing there elegantly. He saw his bulging potbelly, but he also saw his muscular arms and legs. He saw his sunburnt brown skin, his favourite white shirt and khakis. He saw, like everyone else who met him, his receding hairline. But for the first time in a long time, he saw this and he was happy. Trevor slammed the door shut and just stood there. The noise of this breaking the silence for a second, before it engulfed the area again. Trevor knew. He didn't know how he knew, but he knew the man he was looking for was in there. Waiting for him. And for the first time, he knew what he was going to do, what he had to do and wasn't sad or afraid about it. For the first time in his life, Trevor knew what his purpose was.

Trevor walked, no, strolled towards the store. Not a care in the world, seemingly. God's avenging angel, he was, and he would strike the unrighteous down.

The hitman saw Trevor approaching and waited. The stupid dingo had run off while he'd been focussed with Jerry. Well, he knew Jerry wasn't the guy who'd taken him, that was pretty obvious, and he'd surely be back to him, when he saw the real fiend was back. And of course, that moment had arrived. He thought about just shooting the man, but that didn't seem right, for some reason. He wanted a fight, and it would be just too easy to shoot the man, and so for that reason, he let Trevor walk into the store and did not shoot him.

"So, you're the man who stole my dingo?" asked the hitman.

"Yes, name's Treva, and I presume you're the bastard that killed those farmers?"

"Oh, yes, that was me. Not much fun slaughtering the elderly, still any killin's better than none."

"You're fucking sick!…Well, I'm sure you know why I'm here, and I sure as hell know why you're here, so we may as well get it over and done with. Only one of us is leaving here alive, no point in delaying that."

The hitman grinned.

"I see the gun on the counter, no need for that, right? We sort this out like men. You, me."

"Exactly my thoughts, if I'd wanted it any other way, you'd be dead already. I'm going to enjoy ripping you apart."

Before the two men could 'sort it out like men', Bob ran out of the shadows in between the two of them. A momentary distraction from the death that was about to occur.

"Hey, come to me, Santa's Little Killer!" shouted the hitman.

"Fucking hell! That's one hell of a stupid name. Don't go to him, come to me, Bob!" shouted Trevor in response.

"Oh, you fucking inbred swine, you really think he'll come to you. And moreover, you fucking *named* him? You never name another man's dingo. You never fucking name another man's dingo! Come to me, Santa's Little Killer, come to Pappa, you little rippa."

Trevor looked curiously at the hitman for a moment, it seemed even serial killers could love. The things you learn, he shook his head smiling, even though he realised the seriousness of the situation. Bob stood between the two, wondering for a second which to choose, but then, he remembered the former owner, the bad man and knew he wasn't going back to that.

"Come here, Bob, come on, boy." In response to this, Bob came running over to Trevor, to the surprise of the hitman.

"Okay, listen to me, boy, go run outside. And don't come back until he's dead," said Trevor quickly.

"You'll die for this, you bastard! Originally I was gonna give you a fair go, but now, I'm not. I'm just gonna kill you. Put you down like the dog you are. But I'm gonna do it slowly," the hitman growled, reaching for his gun.

Bob looked up at Trevor whimpering, not wanting to leave. But Trevor knew that if Bob stayed, he wasn't going to come out of this alive.

"Go boy, go, go!" screamed Trevor harshly, causing such surprise in Bob that he finally followed the command and ran away, out into the wilderness of the outback.

By now, the hitman had grabbed the gun and was swinging it around to shoot Trevor. Trevor dived behind a row of shelves, narrowly missing two succinct bursts of fire. It seemed Mr Death, Trevor's name for the man whose name he did not know, was a professional. And it also seemed, now, that the man had completely forgotten about his pledge to kill him slowly and was ready to finish him off quickly. Trevor scrambled down the aisle, looking behind him to see Death lining up his target. He wasn't going to make it. Trevor slipped, narrowly missing a bullet heading directly for his head and instinctively rolled over to miss a shot straight at his chest. Trevor pushed desperately against the metal shelf beside him, causing it to collapse, momentarily distracting Death and also allowing him space to wriggle through. He made a mad dash for the end of the row, scrambling over the debris. He could see the back of the row in front of him—across the back lay the drinks and perishables in freezers.

Some innate sense told him to duck and swerve just at the right time. However, he couldn't outrun bullets, and no sense, of any kind, was gonna stop a trained killer from hitting a target a couple of metres away. But he was almost at the back now; he could practically smell the chocolate milk in the freezers.

But he didn't make it. He felt the first piercing pain in his chest, just below the heart. Then he felt a second, even closer to the heart. The momentum carried him forwards, he didn't stop running, well, gliding more like it, but then, he was shot in the leg and he tumbled. He was done for and he knew it.

Act 9: The Sunset

Click.

Then another...

Click.

Trevor looked behind him and saw the man was out. Please God, please don't let him have brought another magazine. But of course, as everything in his life turned out, it turned out shit. He saw the man pull another magazine out of his jacket. As the man detached the existing one and fit the next, Trevor dragged himself towards the back of the store. It was a race against the clock. Would he make it there before the man reloaded or would he be a red stain on the floor? Just as he heard the final click of the new magazine being put in, he made a final desperate heave and pushed himself around the corner of the shelf, mercifully shielded by it.

"Ah, so you're hiding now, behind your little shelter like a little pig. Well, I'm the big bad wolf and I'll blow your house down," the hitman said with an evil laugh.

Trevor turned to sneak a peek at his assailant but was met instantly by a bullet that missed him by inches, convincing him to stay tightly behind the cover of the shelf.

"Oh, watch it, little piggy, you were almost bacon there," he taunted.

Trevor looked to the side and saw the door a couple of rows forwards…could he make it? He knew he'd have no chance of surviving if he stayed here. He knew he had to take the chance.

Well, Trevor thought, *I'm dead if I stay, I'm dead if I run, but I'm alive if I'm outside, do the maths.* There was only one outcome in which he didn't die and that was if he defied probability and physics and outran bullets, making it outside.

"Oh, piggy, I think it's time I blew down your house!" bellowed the hitman.

Fuck it, Trevor thought, *stranger things have happened, as the saying goes*. And so, he ran…

Well, not exactly…because of the injuries it was more like speed limping. Trevor had failed to notice the injuries in question because of the adrenaline pumping throughout his body. As Trevor speed-limped, injuring himself further, he could feel the bullets graze him, as he attempted to both speed-limp and duck behind the shelves as he did so. He began to feel increasing pain throughout his body but ignored it, still running high on adrenaline. He could see the bullets hitting things throughout the shop, the back windows of the freezers behind him shattering and orange juice bursting out all over him. Yet again, he felt searing pain as he was hit in the upper arm, the mix of the wounds and the orange juice causing a scorching sting. Yet he did not stop his speed-limping, even though by now his whole body felt like it was about to collapse. Trevor looked up in surprise. He'd made it to the end of the row and now only had to run up the final aisle under cover. Again, the hitman was reloading, and he knew this was his chance. He speed-limped up the final aisle, but as he came to the end, he could see the chips packets and jars being blown apart by Death's bullets. He had reloaded and was coming right for him. He hadn't made it in time!

Trevor knew he wouldn't make it to the door now. He'd be shot to pieces before he even got his hand on the handle. So, Trevor looked at the window in front of him, and using his legs, kicked it in. He yelped in pain as glass shards stabbed his feet. He hadn't completely finished creating a hole by the time Mr Death was upon him. Every effort he had made ...it had seemed that he had nearly made it...but never made it. And the results had always been terrible. A trend that had haunted his life. A trend that continued today. Maybe if he'd taken more risks, had stepped up and taken action, things would have ended differently. Maybe if he'd stopped his friends, his girlfriend, his brother from doing drugs, been assertive and taken a risk, things would have gone differently. Maybe if he'd searched the village first, the ambush never would have happened. Maybe if he'd taken a risk and said no to his superiors, he might have gotten back up and his soldiers may not have died. Maybe if he'd done what he knew was right and stopped those soldiers from killing that villager, everything may have been different. Maybe the future determined the past, and the past the future. Maybe he had always, and was always, going to not stop the murder of that villager. Maybe it was divine punishment, for that terrible act, that his life should suck. But whether that was fact, or his deranged delusions, he knew if life had taught him anything, it was time he took a risk. A risk that could change his life forever. So he launched himself through the glass and hoped for the best.

Trevor landed roughly on the wooden steps. Instant pain exploded through his body. His face was all cut up and jagged bits of glass stuck out. His arms were a literal mosaic of glass. Glass had punctured numerous veins and he was bleeding profusely. He dragged himself down the stairs, painting them red anew. His eyes welled up and he began to sob. He hadn't thought it would end like this. He guessed that no one thought it was going to end how it did, though.

Trevor saw his blood billowing out through the sand. He wondered how long he had left. Seconds, minutes, hours? Trevor turned over on his back to watch the man who would kill him, commit the act. He watched Mr Death walk down the stairs and look at him.

"Well, Trevor, it looks like your time has come to an end."

Trevor looked up at the gun in the man's hand; the hitman saw this and laughed.

"Oh, you think I'm going to use this on you, well, of course not," he said laughing, tossing the gun away. "I love getting my hands dirty, all bloody and bruised. I'm gonna beat your fucking brains in."

Trevor tried to struggle up, but to no avail. He wouldn't die like this, he couldn't. He wasn't ready to meet the ghosts of his past. Death bent over Trevor and raised his fist, but before he could bring it down, Bob came running out and pounced on the man. Bob latched onto the man's face, mauling him. He gouged out the man's eye and bit off his nose. Death fought back ferociously, smashing his hands into the dog's head, followed by flinging the dog by its legs into the ground. The loud snap of one of Bob's legs breaking rang out.

"No!" Trevor cried out, having watched the whole event unfold in terror.

He could see Death screaming, trying to come to grips with what had just unfolded. His back turned to Trevor. This was his chance, he knew. He felt like he had said that a hundred times today, but he knew this time it was true. This was his final chance. Trevor summoned the remaining strength left in his body and struggled over towards the man. He punched Death in the back of the head as hard as he could, followed by bringing his elbows down as hard as he could on the man's neck. He didn't know which blow killed the man, but he knew that after the second, he was *very* dead.

Trevor slumped backwards after the deed was done. As he looked up at the sky, he noticed it was getting close to sunset. Trevor decided he knew how he was going to die at that moment. The injuries sustained during the fight were critical. He knew it was almost time to rest and he welcomed that feeling. But there was one last thing he had to do, he knew that, but he didn't know what it was. He shuffled towards a tree and rested against it. If he *was* to die, what better place than here. He would rest here in the shade of the tree and watch the sun go down. And with it, him.

As he stared out into the distance, consciousness began to leave him. He couldn't distinguish whether he was dead, alive or asleep anymore. He didn't even know which outcome he wished for anymore. As Trevor faded away, he was nudged by something, that something being very moist.

"What is it?" he moaned.

He began to slip from consciousness again.

This time, the nudge was more urgent, and he turned to see a badly injured Bob. He looked into the dingo's eyes. What he saw in them was a message, the eyes looked at him as if to say, 'Don't go, Trevor, stay awake.'

Trevor looked down at him sadly.

"I'm sorry, mate, but it's time for me to rest."

"Ruff," Bob replied as if to say no.

"Come keep me company as I watch the sunset, for the last time," Trevor muttered.

Bob limped off towards the door, pulling his body forwards.

"No, please don't leave me. Please don't leave me," Trevor cried, slipping out of consciousness.

Reality, or he thought it was reality, returned to Trevor several minutes later, in the form of Bob licking his face.

"What is it, boy?" Trevor whispered.

Bob signalled him by nodding his head downwards. Trevor followed Bob's gaze to see that he had pulled over medical supplies, water and food. In his state, Trevor seemed not to truly realise what they were for. Bob could see Trevor slowly drifting away and barked demandingly for Trevor to take action.

"Just let me die in peace," Trevor cried out.

Bob barked yet again, as if to say *it's not your time yet*.

Trevor looked at the sorry picture of Bob and the depressed look the dingo gave him. A look that could melt anyone's heart.

"Stop looking at me like that," Trevor said.

"Ruff," replied the dingo, as if to say, *not until you use the supplies*.

Trevor looked at the dingo, then the supplies, then the dingo and then the supplies. The dingo padded off to where the supplies were. Trevor dragged himself over to the first aid kit. Slowly and painfully Trevor bandaged himself up, applying gauze and even managing some basic sanitation of his wounds. The worst part was pulling out the shards of glass and wondering if one of them had nicked an artery that would cause a dangerous gush of blood, as if he was turning on a deadly tap, releasing his life with the red torrent that would flow. He also managed to drink; he didn't even know how, every sip an effort, almost choking many times. He knew the efforts he was implementing weren't going to save him, he needed serious medical attention. But at least, they'd keep him alive for a little while. Everything seemed to him so surreal and unbelievable. Like how he'd managed to patch himself up, how the dingo had gotten the supplies and how, when he looked back over at the patches of blood all over the place, he was still even alive with the amount of blood loss.

So, Trevor sat there with Bob in his lap, watching the most beautiful sunset he'd ever seen in his life. He patted Bob gently, as the dingo slowly succumbed to his injuries. Bob took his last breath just before the sun finally set. And for the second time in his life, he truly cried. After this, Trevor was left to sit there alone and sad but more than anything, tired. He was left to ponder his existence; he wanted to rest, but something kept holding him back from resting. He'd have liked to have thought it was God wanting him to live, but he had a deeper suspicion that it was the ghosts of his past not wanting to let him go yet. And when the brilliant ochre sun finally disappeared and the brilliant pink sky slowly dimmed to black, filled with stars, he passed on to sleep. But just before his eyelids fluttered closed, he saw one more star in the sky.

Act 10: Giving Up the Ghosts

Trevor awoke to the sun gleaming in his face and the feeling that his...*well, that was odd,* he thought. He simultaneously felt and didn't feel at all. This fact being too disturbing to Trevor, he chose to ignore it. Another fact that he chose to ignore was the absence of Bob. His body was nowhere to be seen. Trevor got up, easily, yet not, at the same time, another fact that disturbed him greatly. He looked at his arms and yes, they were scarred and bandaged, that for some reason reassured him. He walked, with the slightest limp, towards the store passing over the dead body of Death. A little way from the body of Death was a shape that Trevor did not try to make out.

Trevor walked into the highway store, seeing the trail of carnage from the blood outside the store to the shattered windows and pulverised food and drink inside the store. *Well, the resale value on this ain't going to be good*, he thought ironically to himself. Trevor walked towards where the beer was stored and then thought better of it.

"Those days are over," he muttered.

Instead, he walked towards the bathroom—what he needed was a nice relaxing shower.

Trevor undressed and relaxed as the warm water streamed down his body. It all felt too good to be true, he thought, as the water cleansed his body. Removing the dirt, scum and blood desecrating his body. Yes, he thought, it felt unreal, like a memory. The memory of all the best showers he'd ever had.

As he relaxed, the bandages slowly fell off, yes, there were scars, yet it seemed all the wounds had healed up. Maybe he had truly been saved by a miracle. He turned off the tap and walked out of the shower. As he dried himself, he now more closely examined the scars. *Well, there goes my modelling career*, he thought cheerily to himself. He looked at himself in the mirror. His chest a map of past wounds, his face similarly littered. Though besides the scars on his face, there was something odd about it. It almost seemed too pale. He shook this thought away and looked again and saw his face bright and colourful as usual. *These things happen when you've endured what you have*, he reasoned with himself. *Of course*, he consoled himself, *you won't be feeling right but it'll get better*, he thought optimistically. He was sure the weird feeling he felt would disappear.

Trevor dressed himself and then sat on the veranda, waiting. He was sure something would come; he just hoped it wouldn't be trouble this time; however, based on his current track record, he wasn't too optimistic.

So Trevor sat there staring out at the horizon for what felt like an eternity. Weirdly, it seemed to Trevor that that was not even an exaggeration. It almost seemed as though days passed. That the sun rose and fell. That summer passed and winter arrived. Yet no one came, no car passed. No noise was uttered, no wind howled. Nothing moved, except the sun and the stars. He sat there waiting patiently, but nobody and nothing came.

Trevor heard it before he saw it. The gentle hum of the bus's engine breaking the silence that surrounded the whole area. Trevor saw the large white bus, breaking through the horizon like a ship. As it moved, it displaced the red dust, just as a ship displaced water along its edges. Trevor wondered who would be on that bus.

Trevor watched the bus's slow progress as it got ever closer. Trevor briefly wondered if it was a mirage, but that theory was disproved when it eventually did arrive. By that time, night had almost arrived too. He heard the bus stop and the sound of the brakes doing just that. Trevor thought to himself that if there was ever a sound to symbolise a bus by, it was the sound it made when it braked and did that little lurch forward.

The bus's doors opened and out of it walked 30 or so people all wearing long white flowy shirts and long white pants. None of them had shoes, Trevor noticed, and all but one of them had no facial hair whatsoever. Trevor thought to himself that they looked very much like a cult. But he wondered, a cult of what?

He watched them as they walked towards him, being led by the man with facial hair. That man had a well-manicured beard that stretched from his ears down to his chin and thinned above his upper lip. He had long brownish-blonde hair and a muscular body. His presence and how all the others behaved around him only proved to guarantee in Trevor's mind that what he was dealing with here today was a cult. Trevor looked at the faces of the people behind him. Many of them seemed familiar to him, yet he couldn't place them yet, with most of their faces half shrouded in shadow. He thought for a moment he saw…Alicia? But then, he looked again and couldn't see her.

"My name's Jessiah, you may have heard of me. I'm, well, I don't like to boast, rather famous."

"So whatta you want with me?" Trevor wondered out loud; he knew the man, everyone in Australia did. The cult leader who had nearly brought the end to a nation, the man who still plagued it today.

"Well, Trevor—"

"How'd you know my name?"

"It's on the front of the store, isn't it?"

"Oh, yes, it is," Trevor replied embarrassed.

"Anyways, Trevor, what I want with you is your life. Or better put…your soul."

"What?" Trevor asked perplexed.

"Come on, you didn't really think I'd let you get away with murdering four of my best disciples. You know it takes great effort to cultivate them…corrupt them." He winked.

"You sick bastard."

"Oh, I'm not sick, but I think you are," said Jessiah pointing out Trevor's sickly pallor.

"Not only of the body, mind you, but of the mind. You are a destroyer of man, a harbinger of death. Everywhere you go, despair follows, I'm almost impressed. Almost! But of course, even for me you are repulsive. Give in and give up, if you do, maybe you can for once do the right thing."

"Never…you, you are the true reason for all the despair. My brother, my girlfriend…all the poor souls who I had to kill the past week were led into ruin by you and the Vipers."

"Do you really believe that, or just like always, Trevor, blaming someone else? Look at your brother, even he is now dead because of you."

Out of the crowd, Robbie came out.

"You killed me, Trevor, when you sent me to prison it was a death sentence. I could never get out of it, then, when I got out of prison, I was angry, aimless and I…I got myself killed! Because of you, Trevor, it was all your fault."

"I…" Trevor didn't know what to say, was it true? Was it really his fault? So much in his life had seemed that way, but—he remembered what the priest said. He remembered he needed to stay strong.

"That's bullshit and you know it. You all know it," he began directing his speech towards the crowd.

"You have allowed yourself to be corrupted by this false prophet, this horrible, horrible man. Don't you see the lies that he speaks? Don't you see his black soul? We must reject him!"

"Heretic! Kill him now, he speaks mistruths," screamed a woman in the crowd.

"Hang him from the rafters," another joined in.

"Calm down, people, we all know the proper way. Burning on the stake." Jessiah smiled.

"Kill him now," cried a woman crazily.

Trevor looked at the woman and gasped. The woman looked identical to Alicia. It couldn't be, could it? Now that he thought about it, the people in the crowd looked distinctly like the soldiers he had led. It had not seemed ridiculous only moments ago that his brother had been present, but now…All this flew through his mind in a matter of seconds but one thought that stood clear of them all was, save Alicia this time!

"Alicia," he cried out, getting up from his spot and running into the crowd, which parted for him. But he couldn't find her; was he just delusional? Of course, she couldn't really be here. And of course, Robbie wasn't here, he was in prison. He wasn't dead, he would have surely heard about that. He looked around at the faces and found he didn't recognise them anymore.

"He's wounded," one of them said.

"Yes, like roadkill, isn't he perfect? Killed by his own ignorance, at the speeding truth of Jessiah," another said.

"That is true, Malorie, now why don't we begin? I think we have heard enough out of this heathen," said Jessiah smiling.

From every side of Trevor, the throng of people enclosed on him, hands grabbing him from every side. Trevor screamed and struggled but could not get loose.

"Let go of me!" he yelled desperately to no avail.

He kicked one of them in the face sending them downwards, another he punched in the face. But the more he struggled, the more violent they became, beating and scratching him as they dragged him towards a wooden stake that had been hastily put up and surrounded with wood.

They tied him to the stake, as he tried even more desperately to break loose. As Jessiah walked forwards, he began dousing him in gasoline.

All the members of the group then began to surround him in a circle, holding hands and chanting. Trevor looked around confused and scared, like an animal caught in a snare. Jessiah now chucked a flaming match into the pile of logs around him and it exploded into a blaze of fire. The fire illuminated the whole area, now he could see the faces surrounding him clearly. As he looked around again crying out in utter terror, he saw Alicia. He saw her face, beautiful as ever, and called out for her, completely forgetting the peril of his situation, the reality of it.

"Alicia, I know it's you. It's me, Trevor."

And then, he saw her look directly at him. She broke the chain and marched directly towards him.

"You left me there," she said scornfully.

"I thought you were dead," he said ashamed.

"Yet you never checked, you could have saved me. Yet you just left us all behind and joined the Army. Lot of good you did there too, getting your entire squad killed, does not surprise me at all. That's all you ever do. Kill and hurt, that's your modus."

Trevor looked at her face, desperate to find some response to her accusation, some excuse…but none came to his lips. So he just stared into her accusatory eyes, eyes that were a well of sadness and despair for himself. As he began to choke on the noxious fumes, he wondered if she was really there. Or if it was just a figment of his imagination, born from the recent and current trauma he was experiencing. He wondered if this were all a dream or if he was finally in Hell. If it were the latter…maybe, he deserved it.

"It doesn't matter whether she's real or not," he heard the voice of Yiannis in his head.

"The only way you make it out of this is if you forgive yourself and realise it wasn't your fault," he heard the voice of Father Callaghan.

"God has forgiven you, but now, you have to forgive yourself," said Yiannis.

And so, Trevor looked at Alicia.

"It wasn't my fault. Sure, I should have and could have done better. Hell, there's so much I would change if I could, but I can't now. And at the end of the day, you, not me, took the drugs. I tried to tell you not to, but you didn't fucking listen and then you died!"

"No, you could have saved me. If only you'd come in earlier, I wouldn't have died. And then you left me there all alone. You left everyone, people who needed you, and went off and fought a war that didn't need you."

"It's not my fault, I was scared and confused. And I know, the real you would have understood that, because the *real* you *knows* that I never truly left you. You've always been with me, it's just that until now I thought that was a curse, not a blessing, that I could remember you," Trevor said, staring her down.

And he looked around at the accusatory faces of those soldiers that'd died and again said, "It's not my fault…I should have led you better and stood up to you, but I didn't. But it's war…"

Trevor knew it was time to end this. It was time to run from the ghosts, from the curse of Jessiah and escape. He would not die here and be eternally trapped with them. He could not be another one of that man's victims.

He struggled, as if with superhuman strength, and broke out of his bonds, running through the fire, which burned him. But he did not seem to notice. Alicia was gone, and so were the faces of those he had let down. He looked at the faces of the people that were in the circle, staring at him dumbfounded.

Trevor broke through the circle, running away. He had to get away from these people, he thought, running towards his commodore.

"What the fuck, people, get him!" screamed Jessiah.

So Trevor ran, and they followed, but not fast enough, he was tackled by one of the men.

Trevor kicked violently at the man's face, smashing his face in.

"Get off me!" Trevor screamed.

Trevor pulled himself out of the man's grasp but saw other cult members were blocking the way to the car.

Trevor saw Death's gun glinting in the moonlight only metres away and decided to make a run for it. Trevor got up, throwing himself towards the gun, clutching it and turning before only seconds later a cult member made a similar dive at him. Trevor fired the gun twice into the man's chest and watched him crumple over.

"He killed Dave," a woman cried out.

"Well, then we better fucking kill him. Forget about the sacrifice now," cried out another in response.

Trevor shot two other cult members who were coming towards him, each falling down. And ducked a flying fist from another, whom he proceeded to double tap in the head. He probably didn't have much ammo left, and if he ran out, they would tear him apart. He needed a plan, something that he usually did not do. And he needed one quick. As the cult members were but metres away, he had it. He ran just past the refuelling pump, luring them towards it. Then, when the majority of them were there, he ran even further and then fired three successive rounds into the pump causing it to explode into a fireball, which both decimated almost all the cult members and blew up his beloved highway store. He saw it burst into flames but wasn't sad. As the wood burned and metal melted, he was relieved. That chapter in his life was over and it was time for the finale, he thought.

When the fireball hit, Trevor was both momentarily blinded by the brightest light he had ever seen and deafened by the largest sound he had ever heard. As he came back to his senses, he looked at the results of the explosion. The majority of the store was blown up or on fire and the majority of the cult members were dead, with a few stragglers left behind, including Jessiah.

Trevor thought briefly about the huge loss of human life that had just occurred and wondered whether he was sorry about it but decided against that line of thought. No, he wasn't sorry anymore, he knew what his purpose was. He walked towards the remaining survivors and shot each one of them, most so badly burnt, it wouldn't have made a difference if he'd shot them now or waited a couple more minutes. This continued until he finally ran out of bullets and had come to the last survivor, an unscathed Jessiah.

"It's just us two now," said Jessiah.

"Yes, it is."

The two men ran at each other. Trevor landing the first punch into Jessiah's ribs, followed by a left hook from Jessiah into the side of Trevor's face. This was followed by the latter tackling Trevor into the ground.

Trevor looked into Jessiah's eyes, seeing just flames. Jessiah smiled at him, as if knowing what he was thinking. The eyes captivated him, the flames sickeningly enticing, but Trevor pushed this away. He would not let this man's tricks or evil confuse him, if he even was a man. Whoever it really was, was going to die. Trevor moved his head to the side to avoid a punch from Jessiah. Instead of hitting his head, Jessiah hit a rock, splitting his knuckles and giving Trevor the chance to push Jessiah off and obtain the upper hand in the fight, which he utilised by kicking Jessiah in the face as he tried to get up, blood and teeth spraying from his face. Trevor dived at Jessiah, missing and hitting the ground hard, scratching up his arms.

The two men turned around, facing each other and began a brutal fist on fist fight. Each laying a blow here and there, neither coming up on top. Tackling each other, flinging each other. Finally though, Trevor landed a blow that dazzled Jessiah and caused him to collapse. Trevor picked up a rock and walked over to the man.

"Don't kill me, please. I'm your brother Robbie, please don't kill me." Jessiah's face had morphed into that of his brother.

"Please, Trev, help me." Now it had changed into that of his girlfriend.

"It doesn't matter anymore," Trevor said, truly meaning the words. Maybe the man was really his brother, maybe it was his girlfriend, maybe it was the devil and maybe he was just seeing things. But it didn't matter anymore. It was time that the ghosts of his past stopped haunting him.

Trevor lifted the rock up and brought it down harshly upon the man's head. Then he did it again and again and again with increasing ferocity. As if, by this act, expunging those ghosts that haunted him.

Epilogue

Trevor tossed the bloody rock to the side and knew it was time to rest. He walked over to the tree and decided this time he would watch the sunrise as a new chapter of his life opened, or maybe his book ended.

Trevor sat there and waited. He knew the darkness would be lifted soon, he just had to wait. And sure enough, the sun did rise, illuminating the warzone that used to be Trevor's Fuel and Snacks.

As the sky turned a beautiful clear blue, he heard another bus in the distance, but this time, he knew that it would be all right. As the bus door opened, he got on and walked to the back of it, greeted by what seemed to be a gospel choir, singing hymns. As the bus took off, he saw bright dazzling light up ahead…

***

Officer Garry Walker wondered what the hell had gone on at the highway store. It was a fucking war zone. The bloody place had burnt down and even that, the simplest of the various mysteries here, was still odd. The current theory being an electrical fault—caused by shooting? There was a dead body and dingo out front, which bemused detectives. Apparently, the victim had been on the most wanted list in NSW. What had Trev done to piss *that* guy off? And if that wasn't enough to entice the Federal police to come over for this one, they were sure to come down when they saw that graveyard. Gazza decided to take another look at it, the graveyard. It was all that remained of Trevor's Fuel and Snacks. And as he looked at the signs that allotted the graves, he laughed.

"Well, mate, I always knew you were a crazy motherfucka."

He wondered to himself where Trevor was now?

The Convention Centre
Part 1

Journey

Jonathan opened his eyes to dazzling rays of sunshine. His golden hair was combed delicately to the right, and his brown beard was so neatly trimmed that it was almost just stubble. His fair white skin was manicured and devoid of any scars or blemishes. His blue eyes beamed in the sunlight, as did his whole face, a face very full of life. His body was slim and muscular. He was a tall man, although every part of his body was very firm and defined. His chiselled jaw stood out and served as the best description for the nature of his looks. Many a girl had fallen for him. He wore an expensive light blue shirt, and similarly priced navy-blue jeans. On his wrist was a Rolex and on his feet were brown Brogues and brown socks.

He sat up groggily, rubbing the sleep from his eyes. His head was thumping belligerently. It seemed it wasn't just sleepiness that was afflicting him. As this sleepiness slowly seeped out of him, he became aware of his surroundings, or rather he was bemused by them. He turned around looking at the beige orange sand he had been sleeping on. He looked at it surprised, although one would not have thought its existence wouldn't have been such a shocking affair. He looked out, seeing nothing but barren desert for as far as the eye could see. *Where the hell* was *he?* he wondered anxiously. He plunged his hands into his pockets, looking for his phone.

"Damn!" he screamed; it wasn't there.

How would he get help now? He sat looking out in despair for a second, and then it occurred to him, although it wasn't rocket science. The common onlooker would have already recognised at this point that this man wasn't the sharpest tool in the shed. Although, he certainly was a tool.

"Help. Help me. Somebody…Anyone. Please. Help me." The only reply he got was his own echo.

He got up, dusting the sand off his body.

"C'mon, someone help me."

He looked around with an entitled gaze. A Van Harris was not treated like this, he thought to himself. He looked up at the sky, devoid of any cloud, and wondered where he was, yet again. However, anyone would have thought it was pretty fucking obvious that he was in a desert. Maybe that would be rather uncharitable, so, to give him the benefit of the doubt, let us assume he means, more specifically, which one. Suddenly, Jonathan's chest bulged, his back bent and he vomited a lake.

After having sufficiently emptied his stomach, he found his brain cells returning. He took another look at his surroundings, noting he seemed to be in a wide valley of sorts, jagged ochre mountains surrounding it. He looked forwards at the horizon while simultaneously wiping the remnants of the vomit from his mouth. He watched as the clear blue sky intersected with the perpetual scrub and desert sand. There was no one here! There was no way to get help! He was probably dead! These unsavoury thoughts quickly rushed through his head, but he pushed them aside. His father would send men out looking for him, he needn't worry. He'd never let him die out here. What was having billions worth if you couldn't get your son out of any trouble that faced him?

He decided he may as well start walking north, or at least what he thought was north. Maybe he'd find some help. Not that he needed it, he assured himself, a Van Harris did not disappear, that was for Kennedys. Though they usually found the bodies, and usually it was actually quite a spectacle. Wrong example there, he thought, it was the British who would quietly nod off, or disappear.

We English don't need such an extravagant death; unlike the Americans we have class and are certainly not show ponies! But we certainly own them. He chuckled at this thought.

So, as he began his walk, and yet more cellular activity returned, he wondered how he'd gotten here. Damn, he knew he drank, but not this bad. Complete memory loss, he'd be accused of being an American, or even worse an Australian…or astronomically worse, an Irishman! Not a Van Harris, they didn't drink themselves blind! Had he been drugged? Left for dead? But why? Too many questions, he answered, his head beginning to hurt again. As he struggled to remember last night, he found it cloaked in buzzing white. He could not remember a thing. Something that was all too familiar to him, though he wouldn't admit it.

He continued walking and walking and walking. As he did, he looked around. It was beautiful, he thought. He'd always liked nature, wanted to be an explorer—but Father! Well, he'd always said that was for lefties and broke uni students (usually both were one and the same). But he'd protested, saying what about the old English tradition of exploration. Something that occupied the time of noblemen's sons and wealthy merchants for many years. His father had laughed at him, asking what there was left to explore these days (besides mines in Venezuela, apparently). He also reminded him that the empire and those days were long gone. If only he had been born back in the day, the late nineteenth century, early twentieth, he could have had a mountain named after him and a decent gold mine too (he chuckled knowing that would be the impetus from Father).

As he marvelled in the glory of the great rock formations surrounding him, an idea of where he was developed in his mind. The Mojave! He'd seen it before in films and books. But that was impossible. The Mojave was a nuclear waste zone now, since the Great War. And a long way from London, mind you. He looked at his watch, wondering what the time was, but as he looked at it, he saw the clock hands were frozen. Frozen at 12 pm, 14 July 2033.

That was odd, he thought. He tried tapping the watch, then began thrashing it. As if that would make it work. Well, now it was just a very expensive piece of jewellery, he thought. He continued walking but got bored. Even his passion for exploration and nature dimmed quickly. Though he couldn't shake the strange feeling, the sense of dislocation. There was something eerie about the place, notwithstanding its disconcerting similarity to the Mojave.

He remembered Mojave, who didn't? Taiwan, Korea, Japan, the East Coast had all fallen. On the Western Front, it was no better, the Russians had smashed through the Balkans and Eastern Europe and were being held back at the Rhine and Alps. At home in England…when LA had fallen, that's when they believed it had been over. American troops were being withdrawn, without them Europe would fall, but then, Mojave had happened. Most Allied forces were entrenched behind the Rockies, but Allied command believed that if they could entice the Chinese into the Mojave, they could take out their Army. They had made Las Vegas appear as though it were the US military's HQ and spread misinformation that the majority of US forces were situated there (for a last stand). The front lines had been stationary for months and there were rumblings of discontent in China, so it had appeared to their high command as the perfect propaganda victory to sustain the war. Hundreds of thousands of troops and tanks moved into Las Vegas, he remembered seeing the images on the television; it had been the most incredible, terrifying thing he had ever seen. The Battle of Las Vegas had raged for days; it was said that there was a Marine in each building. He doubted whether that was true, but it was a bloodbath, brutal door-to-door and guerrilla fighting decimated the Chinese Army. But it had come at a cost—they had not evacuated civilians, just like at Stalingrad, the Americans had believed that the civilians, 650,000 of them, would inspire the American soldiers to not give in, as they knew the fate that would await the civilians if they left them.

But they had been defeated eventually, even though they had inflicted monstrous casualties on the Chinese. As he remembered a lieutenant who had survived the battle say, "We'd kill a hundred of them, but they just kept coming. Millions! I remember my corporal saying to me that we had less bullets than Chinese soldiers coming at us. That was right before the final charge." What he remembered most about the interview is the man's hand. It wouldn't stop shaking.

On that final day, the remaining Marines prepared a final charge, trying desperately to provide enough time for civilians and other soldiers to escape. He remembered vividly, 'The Last Charge of the Marines'; they had moved from the West of the city and pushed through in a thrust against the bulk of the Chinese troops. They had been slaughtered, ill equipped, many had run at them with knives. But they had bought precious time, for a few. After this, the whole city had been torched, barely any survived, hundreds of thousands of civilians had burned alive, or already been shot. The smell…he didn't even want to think about it. Many veterans…those that were left (which was increasingly fewer, each day another ten dying of cancer), would remark on that burning smell. Burnt flesh, a smell they could never forget. Many never ate meat again.

As he looked at America today, they weren't the same anymore. Not after that! Not after leaving all those there to die. The flag barely flew…but that was the same for so many nations. What they had to do to survive. As the last US troops fled the burning city, the Chinese Army ordered a full pursuit. They believed they had finally gotten them. But as they sent their armies into the desert, they were met by SAS and other Allied Special Forces trained in desert combat. Ready to ambush and annihilate the invading armies. At battles like Rocky hill, and Silver Buff, outnumbered special forces had wiped out divisions of Chinese troops. As the casualties mounted and rumours spilled back into China, mass discontent began to occur. US forces began pushing the Chinese back from the Rockies, but their command did not believe it. Wouldn't believe it! Still believing all US forces were in the Mojave, in desperation they ordered the launch of nukes, which until then had thankfully not been used. The nukes hit the desert, disintegrating millions of Chinese soldiers and killing the majority of the SAS. With that, the war had pretty much ended. Discontent had turned to open revolt and the CCP had disintegrated, rather bloodily he remembered. The Russians had quickly retreated, though the Baltics to Moldova were still occupied, as was Central Asia following the rise of the Taliban there. The collapse of Pakistan and Iran had made the Taliban one of the most powerful nations in the world. Ironically, the West and Russia were semi-allies nowadays as the Western Allies funded the Neo-Russian empire's seemingly endless war with the Islamic Emirate.

That was enough reminiscing though, he thought; he wasn't much of a fan of history or war and definitely not the fucked-up politics which made England and Russia bedfellows. Everyone had lost someone, even a Van Harris during that war. Frankly, a whole generation had been lost. Hopefully, it wouldn't happen again, but that was what the last blokes had said, he thought.

So he continued walking along the sand, his mind yet again empty. The only thought entering it was the occasional worry that the sand would ruin his shoes' leather. Or that if someone were to come along, he would be embarrassed, as he had not entered the desert with deodorant and it was rather hot. He also began to feel thirsty…not for water. To take his mind off his again blooming boredom, and indignation at having to trek across a desert, he began skipping along, moving side to side, galloping, moving anyway that wasn't just walking. All the time not helping the impression that he was a fool. He was smart, he thought, just not educated. He'd been sent to a good school. The best! He just hadn't cared for algebra, not when the whole world was on fire. Calculus had certainly seemed irrelevant when he couldn't calculate why his mother and sister had died. He tried to shoo these thoughts away, these bad thoughts! He always had these eternal guilty thoughts, feeling responsible for so much. Not that he would ever admit it. Though he'd make classist jokes, mock scousers and the like, he felt guilty. Maybe that was behind his behaviour. They had been drafted and he'd dodged it. He was a Van Harris of course, not a Smith. Not a little Johnny from Birmingham, whose parents were on Social Security, so who cares if he gets his head blown off. *Stop!* He shouted at his mind. If he wanted to think these thoughts, he wouldn't drink, or sleep alone. So he started singing, out of tune of course, but surprisingly or maybe not, remembering whole verses of *Baby Come Back* and *Careless Whisper. George Michael has nothing on me*, he thought unwisely, before humming the *Great Escape,* so out of tune that it sounded like it was a mournful theme from the Great Internment camp.

He continued his indeterminate forage for civilisation, travelling neither south, north, or *any* bearing. His only company, his mind; something unnerving, something that even he himself would admit disturbed him. The whole environment around him statuesque, not a gentle breeze, nor a creak or groan, no flies, no birds, zilch. As this thought passed through him, so did a…gentle breeze blow. All he could think was, 'that was fucking weird'. This led him on to the great intellectual question of what bothered him—no wind or wind? It was as if his uncloaking of some facade had prompted a recalibration of some ruse. He was proud of this poetic statement of his, not bad for a D grade student. As he looked up at the sky, milky white clouds now dotted it, moving ever so slowly. He reasoned his perception must just be off given he'd had a bad hangover. But he suspected he'd probably been drugged with something funky, no hangover was this bad. Possibly that was causing his weird perception. But however he tried to reason it away, a visceral feeling of terror overwhelmed him.

He felt a mad lust, to bolt down to the ground and touch it. Feel the warm sand grains glide across his palm. But he didn't. He just kept on walking. Walking like a condemned man. Not thinking but just walking, his eyes down, watching his feet move, one step forwards, then another. Sometimes kicking up clouds of dirt, sometimes not. He didn't know how much time passed, but he had a deep despairing feeling that time didn't matter anymore. He wasn't thirsty, or hungry, but he was utterly lonely. He needed the bright sparkle of human connection but that seemed so distant. He wondered yet again how he got here.

He may as well think of some jokes for the boys as he walked along. He was the life of the party and such a role required diligent preparation.

"Ahh, yes," he uttered in satisfaction, "How do you get Warren's girlfriend to go to sleep? You use horse tranquiliser." He laughed at his comedic genius, though it didn't really feel like a joke he would make. Then he remembered that it wasn't his joke, but Samuel's. Samuel, he always had great jokes. Like: "What's black and has no money…(no one had guessed it yet; they usually didn't), an African, of course." A great joke? Now that he thought about it a bit more, the joke was a bit unsettling. Actually, when he thought about it, he really didn't like the joke at all. Then why had they all laughed? These were questions he didn't exactly want to answer at the moment. He would delay it for, say 70 years, and if he lived, a bit more, then add 10 to that.

As he looked forwards, he could see two mountains looming. He did not know how far away they were, but at least now, now, he felt he had a destination. A final destination, he thought, it almost felt biblical to him. The mountain, the desert journey, it was rather biblical. Fuck, he thought, if he were to be a prophet, it would be a lot of effort. Though it might give him something to do, rather than party. *Funny that though*, he remarked to himself, he was a Catholic, but it astounded him as much as it astounded others. His family certainly weren't, they were too good for that (religion), and his friends did not dabble in it either. But he supposed if Blair had been one, anything could happen. Strangely, as he thought on his religious affiliation, he felt better. It was the only thing in his life which hadn't triggered a mid-life crisis in this desert. If he saw a burning bush…well.

As the perpetual day continued, slowly he felt the inward feeling that the day was ending. The sun slowly began to set behind the mountains. The last rays of sunlight drifting down his face. A cool breeze moving down the valley. He believed it was time for sleep, even though he was not tired. He imagined it was just instinct. So he walked over to a rock to sleep, wondering what the night would bring. Hopefully, a plush pillow and a nice bed. He wasn't used to sleeping without luxury.

As he wondered what would become of him, wondering why…slowly the bright shining stars lulled him to sleep. Their pristine glow illuminated the dark sky. He saw the moon in its full glory, prettier than any jewel. He even thought for a second that he could see the Aurora Borealis. The unimaginable beauty of it overtook him, and he wondered yet again where he was.

Jonathan woke up, rubbed the sleep from his eyes and began walking. *Walking, walking, walking*, he moaned to himself. *Is this all I am to do now?* he wondered. By now, his egotistical Imagining that his father would save him had evaporated. The bright lustre of the Van Harris name now seeming dull and murky. However, true to his old prep school motto, 'go forth and conquer', he did so. Although whether he was conquering anything was highly debatable. He was more accurately going forth blindly, not as poetic as Lord Byron's words. So, on he went, with every step he took, loneliness and despair eating away at him. He was lost in some strange land. And he would die out here, he thought to himself. He had lots to live for, he couldn't die out here, he told himself. But he wondered whether that was really true. What had he really done in his life that was noteworthy? Besides squandering his father's riches, partying and being, well, he didn't like to say this, but he felt an awakening overcoming him. Being a snobby dreg on society. This realisation shocked him, so he decided to push it away. If only Lord Byron had been as wise as him and pushed away his sympathies and thoughts, he would not have died in Missolonghi.

And anyways, he could justify his existence. He was important, well liked, a Van Harris for God's sake.

"Born of noble mirth," he stated opulently.

But as soon as he uttered the words, he almost choked on them. His life wasn't some joke, some mockery of nobility. *Neither was the nobility a joke*, he thought indignantly. So he continued on walking, aghast, wondering whether his loneliness had penetrated his shield of ignorance, sustained by human contact. As he looked forward, he wondered whether he had made any progress. The mountains still looked so ever distant and his surroundings ever the same. Red rock, orange sand. Sparse pitiful scrub. The paradise had become hell. Some Shakespeare he had become.

The incessant ritual of walking forwards blindly was broken when he noticed the sky darkening. As he looked up, he saw dark grey clouds enveloping the sky. Harsh apocalyptic lightning strikes began crackling. Then he saw it, as he looked behind him; he saw a tsunami of dust and wind. The sand behind him began to rumble and become liquefied. This only emphasised one thought that beamed through his head. *RUN*! And being an 'expert' runner, as evaluated by himself, he reckoned he could outrun the sandstorm. As he ran, he began hearing and then seeing mammoth balls of hail falling. Instinctually moving sideways, he missed one destined to leave a hell of a crevasse in his head. Spirited by this, he ran ever faster but so did the storm. His footing on the sand also weakened as the tremors constantly threatened to trip him over and then devour him in the liquefied sand, which he was beginning to feel now. He looked behind him, seeing the dark grey behemoth closing in on him rapidly. He had to find cover and fast. But where? The obvious question, its answer eluding him. As he searched frantically from left to right, the storm got ever closer. Then he saw it! A cave! To his right! The storm was nearly here! He could already feel its powerful force on his back. He ran towards the cave as quickly as his legs would take him.

He was almost there!

He would make it!

Hallelujah!

The storm was on him!

Fuck!

He jumped!

As he jumped, he felt the powerful force of the storm smack against him. His body was tossed to the side of the cave's wall like a feather. His body then landed savagely on the ground, knocking him out stone cold.

He awoke to a large pulsating purple bruise on his head and the almost deafening howling of the wind. As he looked out of his meagre cave, he saw sand and water swirling around crazily. He was thankful he'd found shelter. He'd hate to be the poor bugger stuck out there. Or the dead bugger, he thought more aptly. No one survives that. Soon enough, he bored of watching the titanic forces of nature and decided to explore his cave. As he walked further inside the dark cavern, he entertained himself with grand thoughts of discovery of some long-lost treasure. Or even an ancient civilisation. He would call them Jonathonians; modesty was not a strong suit. Anything, though, to try and divert his attention from the pain in his head. And frankly, his whole body. He dared not think of the level of bruising that most likely plagued it. Gradually, he began to hear a gentle dripping. At first, he mistook it for the thumping of his head. Though gradually it dawned on him that there was some sort of stream nearby.

He walked forwards, cautiously feeling the walls as he went. By now, it was completely dark. Soon the noise became louder. He felt no thirst, but he felt an overwhelming desire to drink. A paradox he could not explain. His hands fiddled randomly with anticipation. Anticipation of the silky, cold, sweetness of a gulp of water. So, bounding with excitement, he ignored caution and bolted forwards, tripped over a rock and found himself plunging into a hole of water. Jonathan hit it with a large splash. As he struggled to get his head above the water, he found some prodigious force pulling him downwards. Not to drown him, but something worse.

Why was beauty always the devil's tool? he thought for a second, not knowing why. He struggled, desperately trying to get out. Was this the way he was to go? It couldn't be. As he felt his head slowly go under, as he felt the air escape his lungs and the water flood in, he felt a hand. A hand that pulled him up. And as soon as he had fallen in, he was out. As he lay beside the hole coughing up water, he looked for the person who had saved him. But they were gone.

As he lay by the side of the hole of water, he noticed that the water had now become a bright aqua that illuminated the cavern. It was as if it was tempting him to come closer, with its immaculate blue, that looked so—he had to get away from it. He took off his shoes and socks, they would do no good now, and got up, quickly walking away from the water. He could still feel the attraction to it, but as he got further away, it weakened. As the cavern lightened again, he realised he still had his watch on. It was completely useless now, but he couldn't let it go. It was a symbol or remnant of his perceived status that he was not willing to let go of yet, even if it was broken. *There was a metaphor in that,* he thought. As he held his drenched clothes, buck-naked, he continued his despondent walk towards the mouth of the cave, although with each second, the horror of what he had just experienced dawned on him. As did the distinct sensation that something was following him.

He sat down yet again and watched the storm. He couldn't shake the full of horror of what he had experienced. He continuously looked over his shoulder, expecting something to come out of the darkness. He could almost imagine two red eyes staring at him, but when he looked, there was nothing there. He was sure he was not alone, and the fact that he could not see what else was there worried him.

As he sat there shivering, he mulled over these thoughts. With recent events, he started wondering where he was. This question of his had only become more unsettling since he had first woken up in this place. He found himself saying a little prayer and asking for help. He hadn't done that in a while.

"Look, God, erh, we haven't really talked in a while. Haven't really thought much about you lately, or you about me, I reckon. Never really been into that God stuff, not that much. Sure, I guess I believed? Funny that…But fucking hell, some weird shit's going down, and well, they say it's never too late for redemption, right? I don't know if you're there, but if you are, please help me. Please HELP ME!" he screamed the last part as if up at the heavens.

He sat there looking up as if hoping for a miracle, and when none came down, he collapsed weeping. He was cold, tired and scared. So he began lightly humming, in tune this time. As the storm swirled past, he watched and hummed, trying to forget the vicious cold that stabbed at his body. He sat there unmoving and waited for it to pass; he wasn't sure if he could resist the cold much longer. He rubbed his shoulders slowly, caressing his naked body, trying to soothe and warm himself. This did not work; however, as he inspected the bruising and wounds, they weren't as bad as he had thought.

At least he had that, he thought; he may have goosebumps but at least not scarring all over his body.

For the first time, he began to wonder what his father would be thinking, what his friends would be thinking. Would they be sad, worried? He felt guilty for not thinking about them yet. But maybe they just didn't care. No one had come for him yet—but maybe they couldn't? Not anymore! As he sat there cold in that cave, he tried to remember the night that he had disappeared and ended up in this place. But yet again, he found it inconveniently absent. "What the hell is this place?" he found himself asking yet again. He hoped it would not become a catchphrase. He wanted an answer. As he numbed to the cold, he rested against a rock, slowly drifting off to sleep.

He awoke to find the sun shining in his eyes. He sat up and like clockwork rubbed the sleep out of his eyes. The routine he was building disturbed him. He got up, languishing in the warm beams of sunshine. He looked over to where his previously drenched clothes lay and found them sufficiently dried out by the sun. He only wished he'd had enough forethought to bring his shoes with him too, but he wasn't going back inside that cave. That was for sure.

He dressed and walked out of the cave. The sky was blue and cloudless. Everything was as it had been on the first day. As if nothing had happened. He looked out into the distance and saw the mountains. Was it just an illusion or were they really closer now? He hoped it was the latter. So, on he went. He felt the soft sand on his feet as he walked. He felt the scrub brush against him as he walked. He felt the different rocks, both smooth and jagged, as he walked, although the latter caused him some pain. But as the hot sun beat down upon him, he felt beads of bitter sweat trickle down his face. The heat that should have existed all along had finally come. The soles of his feet burned as the sand grew exponentially hotter, but he knew somehow that he had to keep going.

As his lips parched and his eyes began to fog, his sight became ever more haphazard. But he kept struggling forwards, with determination he didn't realise was there. He'd always wondered whether he had grit, it appeared that he did. Even as his eyes stung from the sweat and his body cried out for rest, he kept going. The desert would not beat him! He'd at least accomplish something in his life. As the mountain seemed a mirage he would never reach, he kept trudging along. As the sun attacked him relentlessly, he kept going. As his body temperature skyrocketed, he ejected his clothing from his body. And with one last longing glance, he chucked his beloved Rolex away. It was as if he had left his past behind. But he did not look back for a second.

So, on he went, buck-naked, through the desert. Every part of him reddening, making the old adage of being called a Pom very true.

As delirium overtook him, he found himself on the ground, dragging himself forwards. He yelped in pain as sharp bushes hit his private parts. Yet he kept going. He kept struggling forwards, even as the life seeped out of him. In front of him, he could now see the shadow of the great mountains. So he pushed on. One arm forwards. Then another. With each burst instant pain. He felt as though he was pulling his muscles apart. They were completely depleted with no energy left. But he continued. Right arm forwards. Left arm forwards. And so on. And soon, with one last heave, he was in the mountain's shadow. And as he lay in the cooling curtains of shade, he smiled. He had done it. He had made it.

As he rested in that shade, he felt it sustain him. Rejuvenate him. And soon, he struggled up. He had heard something, and as he looked forwards, he could see a mountain pass. But he could also see an oasis. A pool of water, bright aqua water, sparkling in the sunlight. And next to it was a banana tree, with a beach chair and table underneath it. And on the table were a beer and burger. His mouth salivated; he was suddenly hungry. Or better put, lustful for a juicy beef burger and a cold sweet beer. But as he walked towards it, something stopped him. He remembered the water in the cave and something deep inside him stopped him. He turned towards the mountain pass and began walking up it. He took one last look at the oasis and then turned away.

He took one step at a time, following the red dusty path up the mountain. He took time to admire the beauty of the valley, growing ever further away below him, and took time to reflect. As his vision of it grew ever larger, he marvelled at how far he had travelled. And soon his journey would come to its close, he hoped. He could almost imagine, though. What if he reached the summit only to find another valley? He knew he would just give up and die if that happened.

So, with growing trepidation, he got ever closer to the summit of the mountain. His speculations on what was on the other side had not filled him with any confidence. And, as he felt he could go no further, he finally reached the top. The path began to flatten down and he found himself in…Another fucking valley! Jonathan reacted to this in the appropriate fashion by collapsing to his knees and screaming up at the sky.

"Why!" he screamed up at God.

"Why would you do this to me!" he screamed in utter anguish.

"WHY, WHY, WHY!"

He crouched into a ball and stayed like that for a long time until finally, when one would have thought he had finally given up, he uncurled and got up.

I may as well keep walking; he smiled to himself wiping tears from his eyes, *nothing better to do*. So yet again, he began walking, in a valley ever so similar to the one he had been in. Eerily similar. But soon, he noticed the sides of the valley moving further and further apart, until eventually he was on a vast desert plain. Soon he noticed a floating neon sign, something very out of place. Its holographic lettering stood out, saying 'THIS WAY' in ambient blue lettering, with a big red arrow pointing forwards.

A wave of relief overwhelmed him; he'd found humanity, he'd found salvation, although a creeping doubt began to surface in him. Where was that sign leading him? And what was the place he was going to, doing here? Yet again, he wondered where he was and how he'd gotten here. He thought he was about to find out.

Soon he began to see a massive building in the distance. As its giant outline began to take shape, he thought it looked like some sort of a convention centre. With weird shapes, and glass everywhere, and concrete, typical tropes of such centres. He wondered to himself what it was doing here, just like himself, out of place in this desert. Soon he found himself in front of it, still buck-naked. He stood there marvelling at its enormity. The building, dubbed the convention centre by Jonathan, was of brutalist and futurist design. It had an essentially rectangular structure at its base. However, built up from this were triangular, pentagonal and various other shapes that jutted out all around it, coated in aqua windows and light grey concrete. Jonathan slowly walked up the concrete stairs to the glass doors in front of him. He opened them and entered the convention centre.

Part 2

Waiting

He looked around the lobby, calling out, but no one came. The room was bland concrete, devoid of furniture. Suddenly, he saw behind him shutters coming down over the doors. He rushed desperately to get out, but they had already closed by the time he got there. He was trapped. He looked around wildly but could see nothing; it was completely dark. Suddenly, a door whooshed open upwards. A beam of light protruded from it; as he turned to look, he saw a figure standing there.

"This way, sir," he heard a voice say.

"Who's that?" he asked, seeing only the silhouette of the man.

"I'm Walter, sir, you'll be staying with us for a while. Now come along please."

Jonathan eyed the man with suspicion but decided the best course of action would be to follow him. He didn't know what was going on, but he hoped he'd find out.

As he entered the corridor, the door shut behind him. He now took the opportunity to look at the mysterious man. He wore a full dress suit, like those of olden day butlers. He sported a black curled moustache, which contradicted his silvery hair. His face was drawn and long, his skin wrinkled and old. His physique was skinny, but there was an inner strength in him, you could see it in his vibrant blue eyes.

"Ah, yes, I'm almost forgetting, these are for you."

Walter handed over a pair of bland grey pyjamas.

Jonathan looked at him slightly embarrassed, remembering his naked state, and quickly put them on.

"Now, follow me please."

Jonathan acquiesced, a million questions floating through his mind as he followed the man through the dark grey corridors, Walter's steps echoing throughout the building. It seemed as though they were the only people there. Not *things* though, Jonathan thought, there were other *things* here. He felt their presence; it gave him goosebumps.

"We must be quick, sir, it's not safe for you out here. We'll get you to the room and you can wait in there, all cosy."

"What do you mean it's not safe?" Jonathan asked looking behind him.

As they moved forwards, a light would flicker on, illuminating the way, but behind them, it would turn off. As he looked behind him, he had an ominous feeling that something was there, hiding in the darkness. He thought he could see those red eyes again.

"I wouldn't look too long at the darkness, sir, lest you want to invite it in."

Jonathan decidedly did not want that and looked forwards.

"What is this place?"

Walter, ignoring Jonathan's question, said, "We're here."

Walter pressed a button and another door opened upwards.

"After you, good sir," said Walter holding out his arm.

Jonathan walked into a room tiled white all over. It beamed with brightness everywhere, even though no light source seemed to be present. Again, the room was devoid of any furniture except for one white bed.

Walter came in and pushed a dial which shut the door.

"Not everyone makes it. I'm glad you did," said Walter smiling.

"What are you talking about?" asked Jonathan.

"Never you mind, Jonathan; now you didn't eat or drink anything out there?" Walter replied with a twinkle in his eye.

Jonathan was momentarily entranced by those beaming eyes, which seemed to be dancing with life.

"No, I didn't."

"Of course, you didn't, Jonathan. You're a good boy, right?"

Jonathan wondered how this man, Walter, knew his name.

"Anyway, I'll leave you now, you must be ever so tired. Just one thing though, before I leave. Don't break the rules, sir. Those being, don't leave your room, don't try to escape. So, no exploring, okay? And above all, don't die." He smiled with the last one.

With that, Walter left the room. Jonathan had been so entranced that he'd forgotten to ask his questions.

With that, Jonathan lay down on the bed. Not sure what to make of his encounter with Walter. Equally, he puzzled over the place he was in currently. Just when he believed things could not get any stranger, they did. As he lay on the bed staring at the white tiled ceiling, he was slowly hypnotised to sleep. As had become regular tradition, he wondered as he slowly drifted off—how had he gotten here and where was he?

Jonathan awoke to find the white artificial light beaming into his eyes. He got up rubbing the sleep out of his eyes and walked towards the door but found he didn't know where it was. It wasn't really a door but more like a panel, and now, he couldn't find it.

"Walter, I'm awake. Buddy. Arh." He struggled for what to say, just hoping he would get a response, but none came.

He paced around the room, wondering what was going on. Wondering why he was here. As he paced around the room, he quickly became bored.

"C'mon, let me out, Walter."

No answer.

"Please just let me out, okay. Please."

No answer.

"You bastard, just let me fucking out. LET ME OUT!"

No answer.

"Oh, so you think you're so high and mighty, that you won't face me. C'mon. Fucking let me out. Do I need to spell it out for you? L-E-T M-E O-U-T, YOU FUCKING WANKER!"

No answer.

"Oh, please, please, matey. I'm sorry for all that, please. Just, just let me out."

No answer.

"Oh god, oh god. Please just let me out."

No answer.

He searched rabidly for the door, dashing from side to side looking for it, but finding nothing. Maybe it was under his bed, he thought, so he chucked his bed to the side but found nothing. Maybe it was on the roof, but he found nothing as he jumped up searching for it. He was a rat caught in a trap. God, he was trapped and couldn't get out. The thought was too disturbing for him. He had never been claustrophobic, but he was now. Mounting hysteria overtook him, as did psychosis. HE COULDN'T GET OUT! HE COULDN'T GET FUCKING OUT! He kept searching, trying to escape. A million thoughts rushing through his mind. Few of them sane or intelligible. *Why'd they trap him? How long would he be trapped here for? Who trapped him? Why was he here?*

Why!

Why!

Why!

From then on, he just blabbered indistinguishably, banging against the wall trying to smash through. As he continued smashing his fists against the wall, blood slowly dripped down the tiles. But he did not notice.

***

From a monitor, Walter watched miserably. He wanted to help this man, but he couldn't. He wasn't allowed. And even if he could…what could he do? He watched from the screen. As time passed by, he watched as Jonathan slowly deteriorated. But what could he do? He remembered at first how he would just sit there screaming up at the roof, throwing his bed around. Trying to smash through the tiles to no avail. Then he remembered him just sitting there, wallowing in his sadness. Just sitting there. Was this the so fabled humanity? Was this the great experience? Was this what he wanted? Looking at the chaos before his screen, he found himself answering yes. The beauty in the bitterness. He found himself feeling emotions and feelings he'd never had before. Pity, grief, joy. As the man before him laughed in his crazed madness, he did so too. A symbiosis of emotion. Jonathan didn't realise it, but the sadness, fright, anger and all the other whirlwind of negative emotions he was experiencing were envied by Walter. *If I could just feel*, Walter thought wistfully.

***

Jonathan sat there looking despairingly up at the ceiling. He did not know how long he'd been here, but by now, he'd realised time was irrelevant. He just had to wait. But what for? As time passed, as his beard grew longer and longer, the loneliness and emptiness overwhelmed him. He found himself talking to Walter, even though no answer ever came. And he wasn't even sure if he was there anymore. He talked of his life, of his aspirations when he would surely be released.

He talked about how everyone loved him, how he was the life of the party. How people laughed. At him. How they despised his wealth. How he took drugs, how he was thrown out of home. How his life was meaningless, how he hurt people and didn't care, how he never ever fucking did an honourable thing. How this loneliness was something he could not take anymore.

Soon he seemingly lost the ability to speak, just mumbling senseless things as evermore time passed. Then one day, he walked over to the wall and began bludgeoning his head against it. From the monitor, Walter looked despairingly at the image unfolding. He couldn't kill himself, there were fates worse than waiting. Jonathan would not find peace in death! He had no idea what he was doing. As Jonathan beat his head ever more savagely against the wall, Walter knew he had to do something. But the consequences, God. He'd already helped this man, back in the cave, and God, he was on his last warning. If he did this, they'd...he'd just cease to exist.

"Chamomile tea!" screamed Walter.

His face reddening and veins pulsating, he knew what he had to do. He ran for Jonathan's room, he only hoped he'd make it in time.

Walter slid down the hallway as he rushed to the room. He frantically searched for the button, forgetting its position in his rattled condition. Finding it, he smashed it down and rushed to Jonathan, who was oblivious to his entry. Walter saw the blood trickling down from the wound in Jonathan's head. God, it looked horrid. Knowing he had to stop him immediately and words would do no good, he tackled Jonathan knocking him out.

Jonathan awoke to find himself inside Walter's quarters. As he attempted to get up, he found himself in an art-deco living room that seemed like it was right out of the 1920s. With expensive furniture and exotic wallpaper, his senses were instantly overwhelmed. Soft lounge jazz played lightly in the background.

"Quite a place you have here, Walter," was all he could muster before falling back to sleep.

Jonathan awoke yet again to find Walter treating his head wound.

"Why'd you help me?" was all he could think to say.

"I just don't know. I had to save someone, Jonathan, if you know what I mean. Many a person has come here. Most have gone down, very few up. Some have stayed here for millennia. I...I just wanted to save someone."

Jonathan looked at Walter quizzically not understanding what he meant.

"What even is this place?"

"Look…Oh, what the sunflower, I'm in enough trouble anyways, so I may as well tell you. This place is what I believe you humans call purgatory."

"What…" as the realisation of what those words meant slowly dawned on him, a wave of interminable horror overcame him. He was dead. Dead! He'd never drink again, eat again, no wonder he'd never been hungry. Never another hamburger, the thought made him weep even though he wasn't particularly fond of them. Would he ever read again, watch sport? Certainly not, let alone talk to another human being.

"I don't know what to say, it's…"

Neither did Jonathan who just sat there weeping. He'd never have a chance to make his mark on history. What would he be remembered for, he asked himself. Being just another rich wanker. A playboy dickhead! The thought overtook him, self-pity, self-loathing endemic. Then the thought came to him.

"How did I get here, Walter?" asked Jonathan coldly.

"It's quite a thing to see a man die. Seeing yourself die, it changes a man. Does funny things to them. I don't think you should."

"I need to know, please."

"I can't…no one should ever see that. It'd make men stronger than yourself go crazy. And in your current state…"

"I deserve to know, I won't blame you if I go cuckoo," Jonathan said the last part lightly, even managing a bit of a laugh.

"I'm really not sure…"

"If you want me to heal, come to terms with…you know. I need to know, how I…"

Walter looked at Jonathan. He knew he shouldn't, humans and their emotions, they were rather unstable but very sentimental. Especially about death. He knew it wasn't wise, but he was also intrigued to see the man's reactions to viewing his own death. This growing curiosity of his was sure to get him in trouble, he thought, but then again, wasn't he already in enough so that it didn't really matter at this point?

"Fine, follow me if you're up to it. But I must strongly advise you against this course of action."

Jonathan followed him into the adjacent room in which there was an olden days-styled projector and screen.

"Just a projector?" questioned Jonathan, Walter wasn't taking him for a fool again, was he?

"It can show any event that has ever happened, or is going to."

"Quite a projector."

"Certainly is. Are you sure about this?"

"Deadly." Jonathan laughed awkwardly, trying to conceal his primal fear.

"Well…"

Walter turned on the projector, and both men sat down on the couch as it slowly flickered into life.

Jonathan watched himself. He watched himself party, he watched himself drink, get high and partake in all manner of vile hedonistic activities. He watched that empty look in his eyes. The emptiness that had always been there, since his mother and sister had died. Since his father had started drinking. Since the war. He looked at the image, a tear rolling down his face. He watched himself walking unevenly towards his Lamborghini. He watched himself press down on the accelerator. Speeding down the London streets.

50!

60!

70!

80!

90!

100!

Why did no one stop him?

Where were the cops?

He watched as he neared a curve he hadn't noticed. He watched as the car went over the curb and smashed through a restaurant window. He watched as he lay there in the broken glass, and oh god, the horrid entanglement of bodies. They'd just been enjoying their dinner and he'd, he'd! He'd fucking gone through the window and killed them all. They were just…children. He watched himself, coughing blood and slowly…

"I think you've seen enough," said Walter turning off the projector lightly.

"I—" Jonathan did not know what to say.

"Look, I told you it's—"

"Why'd you help me? Look what I did. I'm a fucking, a fucking monster! I deserve to go to Hell. I deserve to be dead. All those people, God. I killed them. I killed them all."

"Look, sir, I helped you because no one else ever has. Sure, people have flung money at you but never taken time to love you, nurture you. I helped you because you needed helping. Everyone's done bad stuff in their lives, sure you did a terrible thing, but I believe in salvation and redemption."

Redemption, the word zoomed into Jonathan's mind.

"I can undo this right, you know, we can go back and stop it from happening."

He looked into Walter's eyes, seeing the response before any words had been spoken.

"I'm sorry, Jonathan, but we can't do that. What's done is done. You can't just go back in time."

"Why not…Why not, Walter…why not?" Jonathan moaned.

Jonathan searched his mind frantically for some solution.

"Well, let me just go back. Oh god, just let me go. I have money, I can help the families. Please. Just give me a chance to do something good. Please. I just wanna go home. Please let me go back."

"I'm sorry, Jonathan, but you can never go back."

"But…but I thought you wanted to save me. This is the only way. I…I can't stay here any longer. God, I'm such an asshole, I probably deserve this, but I can't do anything good here. Please." As Jonathan began to cry, Walter held him, soothing him.

Part 3

Home

Walter sat there watching Jonathan sleep. He envied the man. Strange to admit it, but he did. He held some humanity that he had always searched for. The man had eaten, drunk, slept, loved, hated, lost, exulted, cried, laughed. He wondered what that was like. What he would give to go to earth once. But he had his duty, a duty he had now failed. He found it almost funny, he'd been created for one purpose. As one of the keepers of purgatory. To make sure that Hell stayed in Hell and angels in Heaven. That no force would ever intervene. But he'd failed. He'd been designed soulless, but somehow, humanity had infected him. Though he was pretty sure that was the wrong way of putting it. The way he saw it, it wasn't an infection. He looked around the room, he'd tried to synthesise the '20s here. And sometimes, when he closed his eyes, he could almost fool himself that he was really there. He wondered why he'd chosen the era. Was it his own sentimentality, or poetic nature? That in those precious years, humanity had fooled themselves into believing that maybe there wouldn't be another Great War. That there would be peace in our time. That there would be riches for all, a continuous economic boom! But that had been a lie. Just like the lie that he was becoming human—or…

He imagined paddling down the canals of Venice, or exploring the Louvre. He imagined himself in the Colosseum or climbing up to the Acropolis. He imagined watching ballet in Vienna and opera in St Petersburg. He could almost hear the chime of Big Ben. But then, the image disappeared and was replaced with nothing. He wasn't really imagining anything, he was just remembering the memories of others that he had rudely intruded upon. He could neither dream nor imagine things, something humans never knew how much they took for granted. When had all these desires and lust come about? He thought back to when the man had appeared. He had watched him more closely than any others. He had felt some strange attraction to the man, a love. He did not know how quite to quantify it. It overwhelmed him. Not sexual, but he believed the Greeks called it Philia. The deepest of all loves.

It had awakened something inside him, and he now found himself doing the craziest of things. As he looked around him at the room, he wondered why he was still here. Why had they not come for him yet? Did this mean what he was doing was right? A very dangerous question indeed. He looked over his shoulder and found Jonathan had awoken. He went to him.

"Sir, are you all right?"

"Yes, yes, but please stop siring me." Jonathan smiled.

"Look, I can't let you go back but you're safe in here. I have books, music and films. Just stay here, okay? I'll be back later, I have duties to attend to."

Duties he had forgotten about and that needed doing. He still had a job to do, but he wondered for how much longer.

Jonathan watched as Walter left and then proceeded to find a book, sit down and read. It was a good one…three novels later and Walter had returned. Time passed weirdly here, he'd look in the mirror one day and be a hundred, although his soul already felt much older.

Jonathan found himself in conversation with Walter for ages. Talking about random things, about what it was like on earth. What a hotdog tastes like. What it feels like to actually touch something, the essence of life. They watched movies together, classics and Jonathan's personal favourites like *Infinity Chamber*, *Lord of the Rings*, *Inception*, *The Good, the Bad and the Ugly*, and all along, it seemed Walter gradually learnt more about being human. Picking up on subtle cues, such as when Jonathan was angry, or sad. But through all of this, a gnawing feeling kept eating away at him. He needed to get out! Get back to the living. An inescapable yearning for redemption overshadowed every encounter, every moment of his life. More his existence, he wasn't sure what 'this' was. When he once asked Walter, he got an explanation that he didn't quite understand. But from what he had grasped, he was in a state between life and death. Everything was there and not. Essentially, the place was here to evaluate those for Hell or Heaven. But it also served the purpose of holding those who weren't ready to die yet until they came to terms with their situation, which, for many, never came, he warned.

Jonathan also asked about what the darkness in this place was. He asked about what was in that water and why Walter was so adamant that he should not die. Walter explained that although you were already dead, you were not fully gone. If you died here, you would go to Hell. He also explained that the reason that people are held in the rooms is so that the devils lurking around do not get you and pull you down to Hell, like in the water. "That is why," he said grinning, "don't leave your room is one of the rules." He further explained that the desert was essentially the big test. Designed to weed out those who were weak and should go to Hell.

As the time passed by, he wondered what kind of existence this was for Walter. An infinite lonely existence, looking after purgatory. He could not fathom it. He mulled over the thought of those destined to be infinitely imprisoned in this place, never to come to peace with their deaths. He knew he couldn't end up like them. He had to leave! He was remiss to leave Walter, but he knew he'd never let him leave. He was too scared of the dangers of doing so and still loyal to upholding this place. He knew there had to be a way out of this place. A teleporter of some sorts. How else would Walter have been able to rescue him on that day? He just had to find it, before whatever was lurking in this place found him. It was a weird crossroads he was at. Not just the fact that he would have to betray Walter, but the fact that what he was doing was, in a sense, defying God. One he now knew undeniably existed. But…if it was so wrong, he wouldn't get away with it. Right?

Jonathan watched as Walter left the room. He waited momentarily and then made the decision. It was time to leave. He was falling into a routine here, and he knew he wouldn't have the will to leave if he didn't leave now. Sure, he'd be safe and comfortable, but he'd be dead inside. He knew what he was doing would be horrible to Walter, his friend. Yet again, being selfish. Yet he wasn't doing this just for himself. He had to make a difference, find salvation. Help those he'd hurt. His justifications fell flat, but he knew he had to do it. That was just the human in him.

Jonathan walked out of the room and watched as the light in the corridor slowly buzzed into action. *Which way*, he asked himself, *left or right?* He decided on the latter, believing that given the place he was in, symbolism may be present. And that meant he *definitely* did not want to go left.

He walked down the corridor, first cautiously, but with every step he took, he felt some dark presence following him. He looked behind himself and saw two piercing red eyes. He started walking faster but could feel the thing moving closer. He began to jog, then run, then sprint. Those eyes moving ever closer, just on the boundary of the darkness.

Suddenly, the lights flickered off, those eyes were coming straight for him now. The monster running wildly towards him. He turned the corner running so quickly he smashed into the side of the wall. He scrambled up running forwards, just in time he saw a red beam and slid under it. He felt it graze a hair and heard the sizzle. *Great, just what I fucking need*, he thought, *the place is booby-trapped now*. The direness of his situation almost made him laugh.

He struggled to his feet and turned just in time to see the devil chasing him get decapitated in half by the beam. Acidic blood spread everywhere, but Jonathan did not stay long enough to see any more of the foul scene. There would be more of them. As he left, he heard the blood-curdling screams of the monster echoing about. Screams that could make a man go insane.

He kept running down what seemed to be endless corridor after corridor. He jumped, narrowly missing yet another laser. All the while, he could hear those foul beasts, those devils getting closer. Their sharp claws scraping on the ground as they got ever closer. He ran and ran and ran. But they were getting ever closer; he saw one right on his heels now. In front of him, he could see a weak beam of light; as he turned the corner, he could see an atrium in front of him.

He ran towards it salivating in the natural light beaming down from the massive glass windows on top. He was out of the darkness, but the beasts had not stopped coming. He ran forwards wondering where to go, where to hide. As he ran, half-looking back, he could see the beast now. It was like a hellish hound. The size of a man, with massive claws and fangs. All black, with large red eyes and spikes running down its back. He saw a pole and ran towards it, having an idea.

As it pounced, Jonathan grabbed the pole and flung himself around it in a circle. The beast landed on the side of a wall, missing him completely. He scampered up the poll, desperately dragging himself up, inch by inch. By now, a whole pack of the fiends had entered the atrium. All eyeing him off hungrily. He didn't want to be supper, he thought miserably. They began attacking the pole trying to cause it to collapse. With giant perilous jolts, it began to slowly bend. Jonathan nearly slipped off following one massive hit but found himself just holding on. He found himself dangling vertically now, thanking God for the strength of this pole. He could see the beasts readying for one final blow on the pole. It was all over. *The whole thing was a dog's breakfast*, he thought ironically. But as his mind churned out morbid thoughts, he saw the second level. The pole had been perfectly bent so that it now formed a path towards it. He pulled himself towards it with all his might slowly sliding, as the muscles in his arms burned; but he kept on going. So intense was the pain, it felt like his arms were about to be ripped off. But he kept going, knowing even that would be less painful than being those beasts' food.

As the beasts smashed against the pole, Jonathan flung his body towards the second level. He hung in the air for a perilous moment, wondering if he would make it, if he had swung hard enough. But he made it, just. His arms left grasping, trying to hold onto the slippery surface. As he was left dangling there precariously, he looked downwards and could see the mad dogs circling, yapping at his feet. Their jaws wide open, knowing he would fall soon and their prey would be theirs. He felt his grip faltering, he was about to fall. Suddenly, he saw the glass in front of him shatter. For a moment, he thought it was one of the beasts, that they had made it to the second floor. But then, he felt that same prodigious strength. He felt that same warm hand. And he was pulled up onto the second level.

"Walter!" he exclaimed.

"Yes."

"Why'd you come? I…I left you. I broke the rule."

"I already told you why, I needed to save someone."

"But."

"Look, I…I don't even quite understand it myself. I don't even know what's happening myself but, but I feel some love for you. Some love for life. A…a desire to be…to be human? A…just, just come this way. Follow me, I can get you out."

"Wait, what are you talking about?"

"I don't know," Walter said, a tear running down his face.

"I just want to be human. I want to love. I want to dream. I want to—"

"I think you already are," said Jonathan smiling.

The two men briefly embraced, each crying.

"Look, we really must go, they'll be up here soon. And they're not the worst thing here. Those were only the hellhounds; you haven't even met the slayers. Not a very cheery bunch, those fellows."

"So, you have Scots here then?"

"Glad to see you haven't lost your humour, Jonathan, but if you saw them, I can assure you that you wouldn't think them a laughing matter. Let's scream, as I think they say in America?"

"I wouldn't start speaking like one of *them*, but I agree with the sentiment."

"Why?"

"I'll tell you later."

So, the two men ran. Down corridor after corridor, ducking, dodging and jumping over beams as they went.

"We might make it!" shouted Walter in triumph.

But then, a red mist began to appear in front of the men.

"Stop!" shouted Walter.

"What is it?"

"They're here."

"Fuck."

"Run, Jonathan! Back a few metres, there's a corridor, run down it and then left. You'll find a portal; imagine the place you want to go and then step through it."

"What about you?"

"I'll hold them off."

"No, you'll die."

"O' ye of so little faith. Look, I was never leaving the place."

"But—"

"Stop, there's nothing you can do. Please, do this for me. Just let me have one. One person I saved. Please. You're a human, you don't belong here. I'm…well, I'm sure God knows."

"But…Walter, I—"

"I'm sorry, Jonathan."

"I guess this is goodbye then."

"Yes, Jonathan, I'm afraid so. *Au revoir*."

"Goodbye, Walter. You know you might not be a human, but you're the best man I've ever met."

The two men embraced, a tear in each one's eyes.

Jonathan ran and did not look back. If he had…

***

From out of the mist, the demon slayers appeared. Their red eyes could stop a man's heart, their pale white skin freeze him to death and their talons for hands rip out his guts.

"So, Walter, it looks like you've finally snapped. I've been waiting for this day for millennia."

"We'll see, Omoroth."

"Oh really? You're outnumbered, ten of us, one of you. Time to die."

"Well, I like to look on the bright side."

"Yes, I think that explains why you're about to die. A bit too much looking on the bright side."

The slayers pulled out their long black daggers. Walter swirled his hands around and two bright spheres came about. They didn't just hire him because of his looks, he chuckled. No, he certainly was not a pushover.

The slayers launched themselves at him, three ran straight at him, two running on the side of the wall, the other straight at him. Walter threw a spherical ray at the one on the left which he dodged, however, his second attempt to the one on the right hit him where the heart should have been causing him to shrivel into dust. As the one in the centre ran at him, he smashed him in the face with the disk, before quickly swirling around to kick the legs of the slayer he had missed and decapitating him with the disk. He then quickly turned the disk around to decapitate the slayer he had got in the face.

"Not bad." Omoroth laughed, as the rest of the slayers ran down the hallway towards him.

This time, they did not come straight at him but surrounded him. Walter, too, this time waited, getting in a diagonal position, with a disk at the front and back.

"Let's dance!" shouted Walter.

They ran at him, but Walter did a backflip throwing a disk through one of their heads as he did so. As he landed, the slayer's body disintegrated downwards. He then threw the disk at another, whose head came clean off, momentarily resting on the top of the disk which had become lodged in the wall before disintegrating.

But he took no time to languish in his victories as he slid downwards, ducking a blow from one of the slayer's daggers, before getting up yet again in the middle of the slayers. However, this time only four were left, bar Omoroth.

They ran at him, Walter kicked one away and tried to grasp for his disk, but as he did, one of the slayers stabbed him in the guts. He turned around, the pain present on his face, as another stabbed him on the other side. He looked into both their eyes, anguish on his face. As the third ran at him looking to finish the job, he moved to the side, causing more pain as the dagger further penetrated him. But that was enough so that the slayer missed him and stabbed into the air. Walter punched the slayer in the guts and grabbed the dagger from the slayer's momentarily weakened grip, stabbing the slayers on his left and right in the neck and then plunging the dagger through the slayer grasping for breath from his punch through the heart. The dagger went straight through the slayer's body and, as he held the knife, the slayer disintegrated before him. Finally, he threw the dagger through the remaining slayer's eye on the floor. Now there was only Omoroth left.

Walter leant against the wall, panting. They'd got him! But he wasn't finished till he got Omoroth.

"Where have you run to, devil?" shouted Walter.

Walter looked around himself, hearing the evil laughter of Omoroth echoing throughout the hallway. He grabbed his two disks and looked around himself. Every now and then seeing a glimpse. Slowly, he began to tire at launching at shadows, his wounds beginning to take a toll. As he turned around, he heard the voice of Omoroth.

"Oh, Walter…Walter, Walter…Ever so impolite. Turning your back on a friend."

He heard the laughter of Omoroth but didn't turn around in time. Omoroth plunged the dagger into Walter's back and then pulled it out, blood dripping from it. Walter fell to the ground.

"Now to kill your little friend."

Omoroth strutted down the hallway, he didn't need to rush, he'd make it in time.

***

Jonathan eyed off the contraption in front of him. In his mind, he held the image of the place in time he wanted to go. The night of the accident, he could prevent it. He stepped forwards, but as he was about to walk in through the bubble, he saw Omoroth.

"Where's Walter?"

"Dead. Well, in the hallway. But very dead. Multiple stab wounds dead."

"You bastard!" Jonathan ran at him but was swatted to the side.

"I'm going to enjoy killing you slowly. It is not often I get to kill a human."

"Then do it," said Jonathan spitting.

"Oh, there is no rush, we have eternity. You and me. Oh, I don't think you'll last long down there. I think you'll go mad so, so, very quickly." Omoroth smiled evilly.

Omoroth raised the dagger, but as he was about to bring it down, a bright white disk plunged through his neck, severing his head from his body. As he collapsed, Jonathan saw Walter laying there in a pool of his own blood, a bloody trail lay behind him.

"Walter, oh god." He ran to him.

"There's nothing you can do; the poison is in my system now. I only have moments left." He smiled sadly.

"There is one thing I can do," said Jonathan grabbing Walter and carrying him in his arms.

The two went through the portal and on the other side was a beautiful sunset.

"Where are we?" asked Walter, gasping for air.

"Hamilton Island."

"You brought me to Earth."

"Yes, for a sunset. The most beautiful thing this planet has to offer."

"Thank you, Jonathan, thank you."

"Do you know where you'll go when you die?" asked Jonathan.

"No."

The two men lay there staring out at the bright colours.

"Do you know where you'll go?" asked Walter.

"We'll see."

"Don't waste this."

"I won't."

"You live for me, okay, Jonathan? You enjoy every breath, every taste, smell, sight. You do that for me, won't you? Who knows…I might be watching."

And with that, Walter passed away.

Watching

I sit there watching her.
    I see her beautiful blonde hair wave in the wind.
    I see her voluptuous red lips gleam.
    Her pristine skin, like a pearl.
    I see her smile and wish she was smiling at me.
    But no more.
    My heart yearns for her, but I know I cannot see her, feel her, be with her.
    I see her walk down the street elegantly, like royalty.
    I see her look at a picture, and it brings her tears, as well as I.
    I see her drive, her strong sinewy arms turning the wheel with ease.
    I watch her laugh with her friends.
    Her laugh a lullaby,
    a lullaby I wish I could hear in person.
    I see you sleeping, my little angel.
    Your slumber an artwork.
    I see you swimming,
    each majestic stroke seduces me.
    My heart aches for you, yearns for you, longs for you.
    Yet you are so far, far, away.

I languish in the imagination of your sweet scent.
If I close my eyes and listen to your voice, I can almost imagine,
I am there with you.
I am invisible to you, yet I see you clearly.
I see you in darkness and light.
Why, oh, why, can I not be with you,
Anymore!
My mind calculates a million scenarios,
if I had done that, acted differently there,
maybe I'd be there sitting with you.
But I'm not.
I see you fall in love with another man.
I see you make sweet love.
I see him hold your warm body.
I see you grow old with him.
I see you raise children.
I waited for you, but you moved on.
Why can't I?
Am I forsaken to sit here and watch you for eternity?
Goodbye, my love,
I say the words and know them true.
But yet, I cannot go.
You've moved on, but I can't.
I sit there watching you, waiting.
But you love another man now, and I am forgotten.
I died and you lived.
Yet why can't I be happy for you?
You walk down the aisle and I drown.
Why, oh, why?
I reach for you, yet you pull further away.

I look for you, but you are gone.
I sit there imagining your face.
I imagine your smooth, unblemished face,
my hands caressing it delicately, feeling all the dimples.
I, I, sit there in the darkness.
In front of the screen, watching and waiting.
But you appear no more.
Yet I am still here, watching and waiting and screaming and crying.
My heart pangs.
My head clamours with wild thoughts of betrayal and confusion and contempt.
I sit there wishing for one more look at you, but none comes.
You've moved on too now, but why can't I?
I'm afraid, so afraid.
I just wish to be back with you, on that summer's day.
On that day when you said yes.
On that day when this whole tragic saga began.
I sit there watching that blank screen.
I sit there dead inside, waiting and watching.
But nothing comes.
Just darkness,
and me.

There's a Man Following Me

There's a man following me. It started about a week ago. It *all* started about a week ago. Though truth be told, I haven't been able to keep track of time for a while now. I remember waking up and seeing two policemen standing over me, which is never a good sign. They were talking about a crash of some sorts, and when I looked around, I saw I was on a metal gurney. Everything felt cold, and it was just the weirdest sensation. That was before I noticed I was fully naked, those creeps, I remember thinking. Perving on my naked body. Then I heard the big one with the orange moustache say, "She's dead." *What a wanker*, I thought, *I'm not fucking dead. Probably wants to fuck me*, is what I thought. So, I promptly got up and left; I swear I caught them staring at me as I left.

I remember running, looking for some clothes and deciding to go into the evidence room; surely they'd have clothes in there. Surely enough, I found a grey jumper and slacks. Wonder what they did with my clothes? But anyways, I wasn't worrying about that then. I just wanted to get out of that place. There was a mirror in that room, I don't know why. But I remember seeing myself in that mirror, among those dusty brown shelves. I remember my pale white body, looked like the blood had been sucked out of it. At least my long jet-black hair still looked good, I remember thinking. But then, I remember my body seemed to disappear from the mirror; it was the weirdest thing ever. The shelves and everything were still there, I just wasn't.

I left that place faster than a cat on a rat. I tell you the whole place had me creeped out, pervy cops and defective mirrors. I wondered if someone was pulling a prank on me. Larna always said she'd get me one day. Anyway, so I went walking down the street, determined to catch the train back home. I remember walking down the street and thinking people were really rude that day. I'd be right in front of people and they'd nearly walk into me, I had a few close shaves there. Y'know people these days are in such a hurry, they just don't give a damn about anyone else. So, after that horrible experience, I knew this day was gonna fuckin' suck.

I don't know what happened, but I remember seeing on the TV that there had been this massive car crash, with ten dead. And I remember just fainting, I don't know why. I remember seeing the images just before passing out and thinking that the wrecked Prius looked a lot like mine.

I woke up the next afternoon, very angry, mind you. Not one person had asked whether I was okay. Laying there in the middle of the pathway. Fucking hell. Do you know what I woke up to? I woke up to this woman nearly impaling me with her high heels. I rolled over just in time, but I tell you, I was mighty pissed off. Didn't even apologise. I had half the mind to go and teach her a lesson but couldn't be bothered. At the end of the day, I just wanted to get home and see my mum. She'd be worried sick by now.

So, I walked down the steps to King's Cross Station, right, and *again*—people pushing past me, nearly barging into me.

I remember screaming 'Manners'. But no one even fucking acknowledges me. People these days. I swear, I was going crazy. I almost thought for a second I was like a ghost or something. See 'cause I thought I felt a guy walk right through me; I must have just been a bit dazed or something. And I swear people would nudge me and go straight through me. And that wasn't even the spookiest shit that went down. I remember right, I was running for the door and then it started beeping and I had half my body in but it wasn't stopping. I pulled myself out just in time. Could you imagine that? Wow! I'm pretty sure people would have noticed me *then*; I would have become a puree.

Anyways, I was waiting on the station when I saw this man. Looked like a big tough guy, right, big bulging nose, bald head. A lot like yours. Y'know, you two look very similar. 'Cept you have hair, of course. Both a bit ugly, big buff guys. Oh, don't look at me like that. Right, back to the story. So, I'm sitting there, right, and this big creep, right, keeps staring at me. He's wearing this black fedora and trench coat. Looks like he's right out of the '40s. Couldn't fathom why he was wearing it, never can figure why big white guys like him wear stuff like that. You wouldn't imagine him wearing that stuff, based on appearances.

So, I decide that's it, I'm leaving. Didn't wanna get raped or anything. So I start walking away and the bastard starts following me. I was like, fucking great, that's all I need right now. I start shouting for help, but no one responds, right. They all just ignore me. And old mate over there just keeps on getting closer. So I run up the stairs and he starts running after me too. The oddest thing happens next, right. I reach the top of the stairs and it's night-time. I wondered if someone had drugged me or something. It was the weirdest thing ever, and all the lights started buzzing and illuminating weirdly around me. Shit, spooky! I see the guy running behind me, like a massive rugby player, and even though I'm feeling shaky and dizzy, I run to the phonebooth. Dial triple zero and get the operator, who goes in that bitchy voice, "Who do you need, Police, Fire, Ambulance?" And all the while I'm screaming.

"Police, police. Somebody's trying to fucking rape me, imbecile."

And the little bitch just ignores me, and goes, "If you don't answer, I'm going to hang up." And I'm answering and going 'help me', and then the bitch hangs up.

I figured I must be high or something, or that it was some sort of terrible dream. I tried pinching myself, but I wouldn't wake up. So, I guessed the former. But I was pretty damn sure that the man following me was not a fabrication of my imagination. That primal fear I felt was fucking real. So I get out of the booth and run across the road, nearly getting hit by five cars. I see the guy following me, unfortunately for him, he gets slammed by a car. But figure this, the guy gets straight back up, dusts himself off and continues the pursuit. I tell you, the look on that woman's face in the four-wheel drive was priceless. Sure though, at the time, I was pretty fucking scared. It was like the Terminator was after me.

Anyways, I use the time to get a lot of ground between me and the guy. Figured I could lose him. What do I do next, right? That's what you're probably thinking. Well, I walk all the way to my mum's place. Long way home, right, 20 fucking k's. Nah, I'm joking, maybe not. Anyway, it was a long walk, I was lost, time passed weird, if you feel me. The night seemed perpetual. Endless dark streets, illuminated by the same lamp. Endless streets, boring architecture. All looked the same. Started to drizzle, like it always does. God, it was miserable. No one about, though maybe that was a good thing. 'Cause the only people I'd seen lately had completely ignored me, like I wasn't even there.

Eventually, I reach the apartment complex; bloody thing's locked, so I'm out there in the cold, freezing my butt off. Or was I, no, I don't think I ever was, even though it was winter and all I had on were some slacks and a jumper. Strange. Must have imagined it, 'cause when I saw my neighbour coming to the entrance, she sure was chilly. Anyways, hitched a ride in with her, didn't even acknowledge my existence. Even Emily was ghosting me, and we always talked. I was beginning not just to be spooked, but generally depressed by this social isolation. And trust me, it had serious downsides; had to just sneak in, wouldn't even hold the door for me.

Bloody bastards, people, don't you think? One minute they're your best friend, the next thing, they won't even talk to you. Won't even acknowledge your existence. Anyways, I walk up the steps thinking about all the stuff that had been going on. Thinking on everything I was gonna tell Mum, and when I get up to the level, I see the door's open. That's odd, I instantly think, she never leaves the door open. So I walk in slowly and see her there, sitting on the couch, crying. Tissues all around her, cradling my picture. She's whimpering, about how her little baby's gone. And all I want to do is go and hug her and tell her I'm okay. But I can't. I can't do it. I call out, but she can't hear me. I wonder if she's ignoring me too, but surely, she wouldn't be acting like this if she was. Has some delusion overtaken the world that I'm dead? Is this some prank that the whole country is in on? What the fuck is going on? I begin to cry and wonder whether I'm really dead, a ghost. But ghosts weren't real I reasoned, but then again, people didn't just not see you. I looked at my mum and was about to go and hug her, but then, I glanced out the window and saw the man outside again. This pushed out all the thoughts of whether I was dead or not. Because this man could certainly see me. He was staring right at me.

I knew I had to run. Who knew who this guy was? All I knew was that he was pretty determined to get me and didn't seem to be letting anything get in the way of him getting me. I tried to warn my mum, but again, she couldn't hear me. So, I went over and kissed her and left, she'd be safer that way, if I was gone. As I left, she looked at the exit in a funny way, almost as if she knew I was there.

As I ran towards the end of the corridor, I could hear the loud echo of the man coming up the stairs. He was fast. I ran to the end of the corridor and went out the window. I opened it and saw the man coming towards me down the corridor. So, I did the rational thing and jumped. I landed in a massive bin, must have broken my fall 'cause I felt no pain. It was five storeys; I should have gone splat like a bug on a windscreen. Anyways, too many weird things were happening to me that even this didn't seem out of the ordinary anymore.

So, next thing I know I'm out of the bin, not even dirty, mind you. And I just run. Run, run, and run. I was running for I don't know how long. To God knows where. I had no particular destination, but I knew I had to just get away. So, there I am running and sleeping every now and then. Actually, no, I don't think I ever slept, I just kept running. Every now and then stopping and just huddling, feeling all depressed, in the darkness and rain. You have no idea how lonely it was.

Just sitting there, looking out in the distance. God, it's funny to say, but it got to the stage where I was longing for that guy to turn up. He was the only human who knew I existed. It was the only real contact I had. Otherwise, I don't know, I would have probably just ended it. Y'know, just given up. Strange, I know. I guess that's just what loneliness does to you. Messes with your mind. Many a time, I almost stopped and wanted to say hello to him, talk. But I was always too afraid. Look, he didn't look like the most approachable guy. That guy runs at you, you run the opposite direction. And anyways, even if he looked like Ryan fucking Reynolds, I would have still run away. Whenever I saw him, something inside me screamed. RUN! Again, that primal fear.

We had some good chases, you know. One time, I remember I thought I'd lost him and was just casually strolling across the Harbour Bridge, then he pops out from nowhere. Catches me off guard, says something that I don't hear and nearly grabs me. But as you probably guessed, I'm still here so I got away.

Anyways, eventually I found you, the only other human that knows I exist. I was walking down this dark alleyway and then this one door opened, shining light in the darkness. Like my saviour. And you called out, asking if I felt like a coffee. And well, I like coffee, what can I say. Oi, what about that coffee, anyway, I'm still waiting. Anyways, that's my story. A fucking fairy tale. Still have no idea what's going on, and I'm not even sure if I want to find out.

***

At that moment, she noticed something she hadn't seen before. On the bench behind the man was a black fedora. Oh God, she thought. How had she not noticed it? Had she wilfully ignored it? Was this the man she had been running from? She stepped back, pushing over the chair.

"What the fuck is that?" she said pointing at the hat.

"I'm sorry, Gabriella, I had to disguise myself so you wouldn't run away," the man said taking the wig off and walking towards her.

"Stay the fuck away from me." Gabriella searched around desperately looking for a way to escape.

"I'm sorry, Gabriella, but you can't keep running. You just can't. I think you know the truth as well as I do."

"No, no. Stop, stop."

"Gabriella, I'm sorry but you're dead. It's time to leave."

The Decision

Comrade Sokolov watched the radar intently; he could have sworn that he had just seen a blip that indicated an American missile launch. There, he could see it again. '*Gavno*', they'd really started it. He wondered why. Why would they do such a thing? He looked around him, no one was here. It was New Year's Day, and the base was empty. He had the sole responsibility of launching a retaliatory strike, no one thought war would ever come on this day. He looked at the blip and saw it getting closer to Russia. What should he do? What could he do? He looked at the red telephone and scrambled for it, dialling the emergency number. All he got was a beep, something was wrong with the phone lines.

He looked at the button in front of him; he knew the protocol. He had to launch the nukes before all Soviet Nuclear capabilities were wiped out, on the first strike. He looked at the red button in front of him; it gleamed evilly. His hand wavered over it as he looked at a photo of his wife and daughter on the control panel. *This wasn't a decision a mere man should be left with,* he thought despondently. As the incessant blipping continued, he got ever more worried. He looked up at the Soviet hammer and sickle and the image of Lenin. He had to do his duty. He looked at the photo of his wife and daughter yet again. "*Dasvidaniya*," he whispered and pressed the button.

Comrade Sokolov looked around himself, slightly dazed. Where was he? Ah, yes, that's right, back in the control room. A room he was very peeved to be in. How come he had to be on duty while all his other comrades got the holiday off? As he vented his frustrations, he saw the portrait of Lenin on the wall, staring at him, scrutinising him, as if disapproving of his lack of patriotism.

He walked down the dingy hallway to get a cup of coffee, looking at his watch all the while, counting down the minutes until he would be off duty. Another five hours to go, he thought despondently. Another five hours until I can see my family.

Later on, he found himself back in the control room with only fifteen minutes to go until he could leave. That was when he thought he heard a blip. He studied the radar intently and found himself seeing another blip. "*Gavno*," he said.

He sat there staring at the button, perspiring profusely. He'd only had fifteen minutes left on duty, why'd he have to be the poor sucker stuck with this, he thought miserably. Fifteen minutes, that's all he had left, he couldn't believe it. As the image of Lenin loomed over him, he felt a responsibility to push the button. He couldn't get an answer on the phone, and he knew the protocol. As he looked at the image of his family, he whispered '*dasvidaniya*' and pressed the button.

Comrade Sokolov woke up; as he opened his eyes, he saw he was in the control room. This didn't fully register for a couple of seconds as he looked around confused, feeling a distinct feeling of déjà vu. It was probably nothing, he thought, pushing it away. As he got up, he quickly fixed his clothing. He was lucky, he thought. If he got caught napping on the job, he'd be in big trouble. As he vented his frustrations over working on the holiday, he continued fixing his appearance. He'd thought it would be a great honour, a great thrill being a government official. Serving the party and state, a role any good Soviet citizen should aspire to. How naive he'd been back then. Nowadays, after years in the service, he wondered whether there was any honour in serving the state, and he knew that it certainly was no thrill. Working in the nuclear section was the most boring thing on earth. You always had to wear your uniform, say the right things, follow procedure, procedure, procedure. As he was scrutinised by Lenin, he finished fixing up his dress, with one last pull up of his dark green tie. He hated the uniform; it was very drab. With the olive-green button-up shirt and dull brown pants, it perfectly emphasised the depressing and monotonous nature of his work. Every time he put it on, he felt a wave of grief come crushing down upon him. He wondered if they'd designed it that way on purpose. He wouldn't put it past those sadistic bastards, especially since it was rumoured that Stalin had been the one to design the uniforms. Thirty years on and he still loomed over every Russian.

Later on, he found himself aimlessly throwing bits of paper into a bin. He'd mope when he missed it and cheer, as if he had won the American NBA, if he got it in. After he got tired of this, he just sat there, behind a pile of empty coffee cups littered along the floor, looking up at the bright map of the world that spanned the wall behind the control panel. Little neon dots showed the borders of countries; he tried naming as many as he could, but he could not name all of the

African ones. Back in the day, it had been much simpler, as many had just been imperialist colonies, but now, a new one popped up every two minutes. This was the only downside of his country's funding of their communist brethren, against the imperialist tyranny. It was harder to remember all the countries in the world!

He looked at the clock on the wall and then at Lenin's disapproving face. Three hours to go, two hours to go, one hour to go. By the one-hour mark, he had been so unhinged by the boredom of his duties that he found himself in conversation with the portrait of Lenin. Though truth be told, that wasn't the first time that day he had found himself talking to a portrait of a former Soviet leader.

"Stand tall and proud, you are a servant of the great communist state," he heard Lenin say.

"Oh, shut up, you're dead," he replied drunkenly, although he was not drunk, just bored.

"Stand, you ignorant worm." He saw Lenin's painted face contort in rage.

"Yes, comrade." He stood up quickly, frightened by the imagined Lenin's furore.

"Why are you not patriotic, maggot?" Lenin asked, his voice turning into that of an American commander, screaming at his men.

"What's to be patriotic about? Everything's *gavno*! Food prices, *gavno*! Our comrades dying in Afghanistan, *gavno*! This job, *gavno*!"

"You show more respect, do you know how many people died for this Utopia?" Lenin's voice returned to normal.

"Obviously not enough, 'cause every thing's…*gavno*!" He laughed at this.

"You impotent, lily-livered, inane, immoral, imbecile."

"Says you. Why don't we go over your sparkling record? You destroyed a country, fucking died on the job. Yeah, how long did you last, two months or something? Managed to get shot by a fucking girl, you did. And talk about incompetent. You starved half the country and literally let the Germans invade, 'cause you thought if you moved the Army out of their way, right, full retreat, they wouldn't fucking invade. *Mudak!* And you call me immoral, you literally destroyed morals."

His rant seemingly silenced Lenin, for after that, he heard no more out of him. Though he could have sworn that from his mantle he was scowling down at him.

Fifteen minutes, he thought cheerfully; he was nearly free of this cursed place. Then he saw a blip on the monitor...

Comrade Sokolov woke up, looked around dazed and then fixed up his uniform. If only he hadn't lost the bloody bet, he wouldn't be stuck here on New Year's Day. He was never much good at cards, always losing. And he would have been kidding himself if he was going to win this one time. So, he'd decided to bring cards with him this time. He'd show them, next time something like this came around he'd be a fucking pro. After getting his coffee, he sat down at a little wooden table. It wasn't regulation but no one would know, especially as...with a mischievous grin he turned to the security camera. Its rectangular shape all normal. Its red spherical light still on. But across the camera's lens was a sticker of the Soviet state emblem.

"Hee-hee," he sniggered like a naughty child.

Briefly he considered any possible repercussions that could occur. Of course, he could deny it, he laughed at that. Even if you were innocent, you were guilty, if accused, here.

Maybe if he was actually guilty and pleaded his innocence, it might work the opposite way; he'd have to wait and see.

But anyways, he found himself not caring if there were any repercussions. Of course, he could be fired, but he really didn't care anymore. And of course, he could be fired literally, against a wall. He found himself thanking whoever communists were supposed to pray to, maybe Marx, that the days of the purges were over. Though those times constantly threatened to return. Not for a second did he think of the repercussions on his family, which he felt guilty for only moments later. Fine, he decided the consequences would be far worse if the camera was covered then if they saw him playing cards. He took off the sticker reticently and made a pleading sign to whoever may watch the feed to forget about the little misdemeanour he had committed.

Well, time's a wastin', he thought, imitating the American cowboy's accent; better start learning to master cards. He also, again, felt grateful that the Soviets had not invented thought police yet, because they certainly wouldn't like him, well, even *knowing* the term 'thought police', let alone mimicking John Wayne. As he wondered how long he had left, he realised time certainly wasn't awastin', as he was only thirty-five minutes into his ten-hour shift. Of course, he got this time off the wall clock, to his left, as like most Soviet machines, his watch wasn't working.

So he began practising his poker face, card arrangements and choosing when to play his cards. He focussed mainly on Durak, although he did try to develop his skills across a variety of the card games. Even Go Fish, because he reckoned the game was more obscure in Russia, so even if he was only half-decent, he would absolutely smash all his comrades at it.

Although he didn't really think this through, given Go Fish is a purely luck-based game, with no skills required. What he was essentially doing, as he later realised, was equivalent to trying to become a master at noughts and crosses. Utterly pointless.

As time passed on, and very slowly, as he noted himself, it gradually came to twenty minutes before he could escape the gulag. Sure, it wasn't a gulag, he'd never been to one. Though his father had. But it was probably just as bad. Fine, a little bit of hyperbole, but Marx, this place was bad. Oh my Marx, this place was bad. Having earlier solved the philosophical query of who communists should pray to, it had been a close race between Marx and Satan. He laughed at that, although a cynic, he thought in reflection, he did still consider himself a communist. Though he wasn't sure if that would last for much longer. He wondered if it was really communist patriotism, or just Russian patriotism. He increasingly believed it to be the latter, though not originally. Sure, like most Russian youths, he'd started off as a fervent socialist, but after he'd experienced what he'd experienced, everything about the USSR, every loyal propaganda poster or song that had once electrified his spirit, just seemed like utter puffery. But he was still a Russian, and he still hated the West. And he still loved the national anthem, though Vasya, the Cornflower no longer roused him, the Soviet anthem sure as (he didn't think a 'good communist' said 'hell' so he quickly thought of a communist substitute) 'capitalism' inspired him. From the first word, so beautiful. He turned the radio on, wondering if he could catch a glimpse of it, it was nearly midnight and they usually played it around now.

Fifteen minutes left, he smiled gratefully. Almost there. But for some reason, it felt as if he wasn't almost there. He looked at the photo of his wife and daughter...

He woke up, sat up, fixed his dress, complained as usual, and was scrutinised by Lenin's eyebrows. He walked down the corridor, every step he made, echoed around the empty corridor. Could it be any more depressing? Couldn't they get a good interior designer and at least pay the power bill, he asked looking at the ceiling lights that were flickering on and off. He remembered all those old Soviet propaganda ads, in which they had beautiful buildings. And smiling children. And shops filled to the brim with the most beautiful produce. No, that was all a lie. He stopped and pointed up at the flickering light, as if he was delivering an American stand-up monologue. So, pointing up at the flickering light, he said ostentatiously, "This should be the fucking ad. Just this flickering light. That is, in one image, communist Russia." He could almost imagine himself, there in front of the bright lights, with the audience. He'd dreamed as a kid of being a late-night host, of going to New York, of hosting his own show. 'The Workers' Late Shift' he would have called it. In his mind, he could see it. He could see the band opening up with a jazzy version of the national anthem, and then he would walk out into thunderous applause. And he'd open up with 'hello, comrades'.

He could see it very clearly now. He'd even imagined a running segment the show could have, called Lil' Stalin. In it, Stalin was a little cute baby, in a white diaper, with his little cap and of course his famous moustache. In the segment, Lil' Stalin would get angry at current things happening in Russia and order the purging of the people responsible. But unfortunately for Lil' Stalin he was only a baby and the only thing he could purge would be his bowels, which would happen each episode.

However, these dreams of his had always been shot down, even from birth. Firstly, he'd had the misfortune to be born the son of a traitor. His father had been accused of helping the Nazis during the Great Patriotic War. Whether it was true or not did not matter, because Stalin had thought it true. Even though Stalin never knew his father or had even heard of him. His father had taken the trouble to get his wife pregnant just before he left, determined that his family tree should not die out. *Bastard!* he thought, spitting on the floor, but quickly recanting this, realising if his father had not done this, he would not have been born. He had been born in the winter of '46; his mother had died giving birth. So, after that, he had been left to the system to be raised in a Soviet institution. He had been given the name Comrade by a plain-faced bored official, who still seemingly had retained a sense of humour, even after all the horrors of the purges (all six billion of them), the war, the civil war, the civil war before that, the other war and so on. It hadn't been the best of times for Russia. He'd hated that official for many years, being called Comrade, bullied by all the children. The only friends he had were his imaginary communist heroes, Lenin, Stalin, Marx, even Mao. He would imagine great fantasies, such as the evil Trotsky rising from the dead and only he being able to kill the traitor. But in the end, as much as the name got him bullied, it led to him getting promoted and gaining positions the son of a traitor would never have gotten. Having a name like Comrade made you a poster boy for communism. In addition to this, as he got older and got tasks like the one he was currently doing, he began to understand that official.

He thought more of his childhood, something he hadn't done in a long time. He remembered being born, no, he didn't. He remembered his early years, no, he didn't. Fine, he thought peevishly, what did he remember? Well, he remembered when he was seven years old, a young grim-faced soldier had walked into his dormitory and called for Comrade Sokolov. All the children had started laughing, and he had told them to shut up with such fierceness that they did. He had raised his bony little arm and said, "Yes, comrade, this is me." He had told him to follow him. When he had walked out of the room, he could see in the soldiers' eyes that something was wrong. The soldier had taken him into an empty room, sat him down and, crouching beside him, had told him that his father was dead. He told him that he had been the one to shoot him. He told him that his father had finally heard about the death of his mother and decided he needed to escape so he could help his son. He handed him the letter which said as much; he apologised that he had already opened it. He told him that his father had made him pledge, as he lay there bleeding out on the snow, that he would give it to him.

He remembered just sitting there staring at a letter from a dead father he had never gotten to know. Wondering whether he should be sad, how he should react. But no emotions could come. He just sat there with an empty look in his eyes.

From that day on, the young soldier would come in and check on him. Making sure everyone treated him right, making sure that he was fed properly, giving him things. One day, he had told him he would adopt him, that he could live with him. He showed him a picture of his wife and three daughters. They looked like the most beautiful family ever. So, he had waited at the front steps for two hours for the young soldier to come, but he never did. He had cried for a week; he never saw the soldier again. He had wondered where the young soldier had gone, why he had deserted him. Later on, he had found out that he had been purged, along with his whole family. The young soldier had made the mistake of saying that he was unhappy, that there was less food in the grocery that week.

He had completely forgotten his train of thought, oh yes, he was thinking about why his dream of being a late-night host never came to be. Well, secondly, the Soviet government wasn't a fan of having a late show and finally it was just him. He was nondescript, like his name Comrade, generic. Generic slick black hair. Generic round face, blue eyes, pale white skin. Depressed look, no facial hair, high forehead, triangular jaw, skinny body. No one took a second look at him. He certainly wasn't very attractive; it was a wonder he got his wife, who was absolutely beautiful.

A large bang shocked him out of his reminiscence. Yet another horrid thing they couldn't even get right, the electrics, he thought, shaking his head. Hours later, he sat looking at a screen with a blip going on and off. He sat there, hours later, mulling over his duty to a state that he wasn't sure he even loved anymore. Hours later, he pressed a button.

Comrade Sokolov, like clockwork, woke up dazed and confused, got dressed, complained like only an annoyed Russian could, and was criticised by Lenin's glare. As he walked out of the room to get a coffee, before practising cards, he felt an extreme tugging at his chest. No, it wasn't a tugging, more like butterflies in the stomach. He pushed this feeling aside as he walked down the corridor. After stopping for an indeterminate amount of time, reflecting on his life and critiques of a system that, at the end of the day he was still loyal too, even though he did not know why, he made it to the coffee machine.

But as with everything in the Soviet Union, it was shit. The coffee and the machine. The machine was more like a water dispenser. So, as he put the plastic cup under the tap and pushed the button, waiting for some tepid coffee, he stared intently at the khaki wall in front of him. The paint was literally peeling off in many places. He wondered who the fool was that was responsible for the interior design of these buildings. He'd been inside one government building once where the walls were the colour maroon. Maroon, *mudak*, absolute *mudak*. Why'd they get the village idiot to do the designing, he couldn't figure it out. But then, he thought longer, and considered the possibility that maybe they were just choosing the cheapest option; he was pretty sure maroon wasn't a very in-demand colour.

Having been so engrossed in his thoughts, he did not notice that his cup was full.

"*Gavno!*" he shouted.

He pulled away, annoyed he'd gotten coffee all over his hands. He looked for some tissues but found none. So he put his coffee on the ground and rubbed his hands against the wall. No one would notice. It wasn't like the walls were kept up. It'd add character he thought, looking at the hundreds of other stains and blemishes along the wall.

He grabbed his cup and began drinking the insipid, feeble attempt for a coffee. He struggled to keep it down but knew he had to drink it; it was going to be a long day. He got back, played cards and then eventually went back for another coffee, and another and another, even as the coffee got progressively colder, until it was stone cold. He wondered why, but the coffees were strangely addictive. Each time he would finish one, he would toss the empty cup behind him. The word sustainable had never entered his vocabulary.

Eventually, he sat there at the control panel, so high on coffee, that he was willing to press a red button. He wondered briefly whether he was properly capable of making a decision at a time like this, but he had his duty. A duty he had thought a lot about, that day. "*Dasvidaniya*," he whispered, taking one last drag of the awful coffee and one last look at the picture of his wife and daughter before pressing the red button.

Comrade Sokolov woke up and looked around himself, startled. It felt like he'd done this many hundreds of times, but that couldn't be. He looked at the photo of his wife and daughter, just wanting to be with them, not with *him*, he thought, as he looked at Lenin's portrait. He pushed that thought away and returned to his usual ritual. Many coffees and card games later, he found himself wandering the corridors of the building. He almost wished for a nuclear war, at least it would give him something to do. As he walked down endless corridors that all looked the same, he came across a brown door. This was nothing special, as all the doors were brown, but he decided he might as well have a look inside this one.

Inside was a chess table; there was one little plush seat in the room, so he pulled it over and decided he would play himself. He had learnt the game back in the day and had actually been pretty good. So, he sat down and made his first move when he heard a voice; he raised his head and saw a portrait of Stalin.

"How rude, you didn't ask me if I wanted to play."

"Sorry, comrade."

"Back in the day, I would have had you purged for that insult."

"Well, would you like to play?"

"No! I am the greatest chess player in history! And the future! Playing you is beneath me."

He decided to ignore Stalin after that, which seemed to keep him silent enough. However, whenever he would look up, he would see those eyes plotting, as if he was getting ready to stick a knife into him. There was something about that steely gaze. It said 'I'm thinking of a million ways to destroy your life and murder you' like nothing else.

He almost laughed, but cut it short, not wanting to provoke Stalin's painting. What great company he had, Stalin. Ha! Soon though, he found playing himself in chess to be vapid and promptly left the room, leaving Stalin in the darkness. As he liked it, he thought to himself, imagining he could hear Stalin shouting at him in the distance.

Later on, he would be sitting staring at a red button, red for communism, he briefly reflected on the symbolism, before he pushed it.

Comrade Sokolov awoke dazed and confused. Not only was it the intense feeling of déjà vu that seemed to just be on the tip of his tongue, but it was also the fact that the first thing he saw was the portrait of Vladimir Lenin. He could attest to the fact that seeing that goatee and egg-like face first thing, took you off guard and left you rattled. The portrait was like the Mona Lisa, the eyes following you everywhere you went. That look making sure you behaved like a good communist.

Many coffees, card games and even a dabbling of chess later, he found himself lying on the ground. He still had four hours to go, he thought miserably, playing with his hair frustratedly. He turned his head to the side and saw a marble bust of Marx. He sure looked peaceful and comfortable, he thought. "Not bored and lonely like me," he continued, complaining out loud as if someone would hear.

He lay there, juiced up on many coffees, and began to think on his loyalty to communism. He had no idea why. He guessed being surrounded by hammers and sickles made you do that. As he looked up at the water-stained ceiling, he thought about the faults of capitalism and America. He thought of their imperialistic 'invasions' of Korea and Vietnam. He thought of the amoral American state, not noticing the irony. For all that had happened to him, for all the wrongs committed against himself, for some reason, he found himself still loyal to the state. Though the cracks, like in the ceiling, were very visible, what else was there? What else in his life, besides his family, did he have?

Hours later, he would be using this, this loyalty he had, to justify pressing the red button.

Comrade Sokolov woke up. Comrade Sokolov pushed the button. Comrade Sokolov woke up. Comrade Sokolov pushed the button…The case could be displayed in a science textbook for cause and effect.

Comrade Sokolov woke up and the day played out as usual. He played cards, talked to paintings, drank too much crap coffee and thought to himself philosophically. With forty-five minutes left until he could leave, he drank one last coffee, while standing at the telephone terminal. He looked at the room; it always amazed him, all those wires. As he left the room, he chucked his coffee behind him, as he always did, not noticing there was still some liquid in it and that he had just thrown it onto some wires which promptly short-circuited, cutting all the phone lines.

Fifteen minutes later, he sat there staring at a monitor at which he thought he had just seen a blip. "*Gavno*," he uttered the words familiarly, the Americans had finally done it. He had seen the blip again. But why had the Americans let loose? And as usual, he didn't think on that question for as long as he should have. He tried the red phone and found it not working, as had been the case for the past thirty minutes, because of him. As he sat there sweating, thinking on what he should do, as he had done many times before, he felt as though he had fallen into a dark gaping hole that he couldn't get out of. Petrified, unable to come up with the simple way to get out, all he had to do was lift the cover and let the sunshine in. It was on the tip of his tongue.

As he sat there engulfed in déjà vu, the red button gleamed evilly up at him. He found himself remembering the old Slavic devils the boys would whisper about at night. A chort! As he looked at the red button, he could almost imagine it was the red of the chort's eye. An unsettling feeling waved over him. He'd been here before. What was this?

He'd heard stories that chorts liked to revel in the suffering of others, that they fed on situations in which many would die. He'd heard that they could even create time loops and that if you ever found yourself in one, you knew you were about to die, or many others were going to. His hand wavered over the button. Could it be? But if he was stuck in one, that didn't mean that the American nukes weren't real. But as he slowly thought about it, as if for the first time, it dawned on him, that it simply didn't make sense. Why would the Americans launch nukes at Russia? They had no reason. He looked up at the image of Lenin, it was as if it was willing him to push the button. But then, he looked at the image of his wife and daughter and pulled away.

He watched slowly as the blip got ever closer. The tension mounted; as it got ever closer, he got ever more tempted. But with four minutes left, it finally reached Moscow, but nothing happened. He closed his eyes, thanking Marx. And saw on the monitor the blip going back towards the USA. It must have been some technical glitch. So, he got up happily and danced out of the room; he'd escaped. He couldn't prove it, not even to himself. But he felt like he'd just escaped some perpetual prison. As he went down the stairs, he passed the man to relieve him; they exchanged the customary comrade and then went their separate ways. But just as he was about to exit, he remembered the blipping hadn't stopped, the man wouldn't know the difference.

"*Gavno!*" he screamed, running up the stairs only hoping he'd make it up in time.

As he ran to the control room, he shouted for the man not to press the button, but it was as if he could not hear him. As he made it to the room, he saw him getting ready to press the button. But when he looked again, it wasn't a man getting ready to press the button but a chort.

"You."

He got no reply as the monster looked at him momentarily; he launched himself at it but…

Comrade Sokolov woke up, dazed and confused. He fixed his clothes up under the watchful eye of Lenin. All the while complaining about getting the bloody holiday on duty. If only he was better at cards, he moaned. But he'd fix that. He'd have eternity, he said. Not noticing what he'd just uttered, he walked down the familiar corridor, downing coffee after coffee and thinking about his life. His former ambitions and his loyalty to the Soviet Union.

Finally, he sat there, in a chair. He sat there seeing a blip on the screen and not believing it. Behind him was a littering of empty cups and a coffee table with cards lain across it. Along the wall was the map of the world, its neon circles mesmerised him momentarily. *All gone*, he thought, *all those countries would be gone. Why'd the Americans go and start it?*

He looked over at the radio smiling, it had stopped being static and, and well, the Soviet national anthem had just come on. Filled up with pride, slightly confused from all the coffee and egged on by Lenin's portrait, he pushed his hand down, not before looking at the portrait of his wife and daughter whispering '*dasvidaniya*'.